D1528065

Contents

Chapter 1

R uth's steady hands poured molten wax into the mold. The familiar scent of beeswax and cinnamon filled her workshop, but not even the comforting aroma could quell the anxiety bubbling in her chest. In just a few days, the Christmas market would begin.

The market her best friend Sarah was pestering her to participate in.

Setting down the pot, Ruth closed her eyes and took a deep breath. The winter sun had barely peeked over the horizon, casting a soft glow through the workshop's lone window. She'd woken before dawn, unable to sleep with thoughts of the market swirling in her mind.

"*Gott*, give me strength," she whispered, her fingers absently fidgeting with her apron strings.

Ruth moved to her worktable, carefully arranging an assortment of candles. Each one was a work of art, crafted with care and imbued with scents that evoked memories of home, family, and faith. Her fingers traced the simple designs she'd carved into the wax: delicate snowflakes, graceful pine branches, and festive holly leaves.

While she worked, Ruth's mind drifted to the upcoming market. The thought of standing behind a booth, surrounded by strangers, made her stomach churn.

Oh, she'd know some of them, of course, from her community. But a market that big would draw *Englisch* and Amish alike, from across the county and beyond.

What if no one liked her candles? What if she froze up when customers tried to speak with her?

Maybe it was better to keep supplying vendors in town who sold her candles for a cut of the profits. It would be easier, certainly.

A soft knock at the door startled her from her thoughts. "*Kumm* in," Ruth called, her voice barely above a whisper.

Sarah Fisher's cheerful face appeared in the doorway. "*Gut* morning, Ruth! I thought I might find you here."

Ruth managed a small smile. "*Gut* morning, Sarah. You're up early."

"Not as early as you," Sarah teased, stepping into the workshop. Her eyes widened as she took in the array of candles. "Oh, Ruth, these are *Wunderbar*! You'll sell out of these for sure at the market." She paused, fixing her friend with a pointed look. "You *are* going to sell at the market, *jah*?"

Ruth's smile faltered. "I... I don't know, Sarah. There will be so many people there."

Sarah's expression softened. "I know it's not easy for you but think of how many people would love to have your candles in their homes. You have such a gift, Ruth."

Ruth's cheeks flushed at the compliment. She picked up a candle, running her thumb over the smooth surface. "*Danki*, Sarah. But I'm not sure I can handle all the... interaction. With strangers."

"What if you didn't have to do it alone?" Sarah asked with a hint of excitement in her voice.

Ruth looked up, curiosity piqued despite her reservations. "What do you mean?" If Sarah was there, then maybe...

"Well," Sarah began, her eyes twinkling, "I was thinking. My *bruder*, Daniel, he's planning to sell some of his woodwork at the market. What if you two shared a booth?"

Ruth's heart skipped a beat at the mention of Daniel Fisher. She'd seen him at Sunday singings and community gatherings, always from afar.

He was outgoing and charismatic – everything she wasn't. The thought of working alongside him was exciting.

And terrifying.

"I... I don't know," Ruth stammered, her fingers once again finding her apron strings. "I'm sure Daniel wouldn't want to be saddled with someone like me. I'll scare off the customers," she joked in a weak voice.

Sarah shook her head emphatically. "*Nee*, Ruth, don't say that. Daniel would be lucky to have you as a partner. Your candles and his woodwork would complement each other perfectly." She clapped. "*Ach*! He could make display cases or trays for the candles, I bet. Then, you can sell them as gift sets!"

Ruth bit her lip, considering the idea. It was true that having someone else there might make things easier. And Daniel's outgoing nature could help draw customers to their booth.

But the thought of spending so much time with him was both appealing and scary in equal measure. Being there all day next to him, having to talk and interact... or in her case, attempt to.

She'd bore him to tears, wouldn't she?

"I'll think about it," Ruth said finally, her voice barely audible.

Sarah beamed. "That's all I ask. Just promise me you'll give it real thought, okay? Don't let fear hold you back from sharing your beautiful work with others."

Ruth nodded, her gaze drifting back to the candles on her table. Each one represented hour upon hour of skill and practice, of pouring her heart and soul into her craft. Didn't she owe it to herself to at least try?

As Sarah prepared to leave, Ruth felt a sudden urge to seek guidance. "Wait," she said, surprising herself with the firmness in her voice. "Before you go, would you... would you pray with me?"

Sarah's expression softened. "Of course, Ruth."

The two young women bowed their heads, and Ruth began to pray silently. *Gott, please guide me. Show me the path You would have me take. Give me the strength to overcome my fears and the wisdom to know Your will.*

As the prayer ended, Ruth felt a sense of calm wash over her. She looked up at Sarah, a small but genuine smile on her face.

"I'll do it," she said softly. "I'll talk to Daniel about sharing a booth."

Sarah's face lit up with joy. "Oh, Ruth, that's *Wunderbar*! I just know this is going to be amazing for you. Both of you," she added with a grin.

After Sarah left, Ruth returned to her candles, her mind swirling with a mix of emotions. Anxiety still gnawed at her, but there was something else too – a tiny spark of excitement, of possibility.

As she worked, Ruth found herself imagining what it might be like to share a booth with Daniel. Would he appreciate her candles as much as Sarah did? Would his woodwork truly complement her creations? And how would she manage to speak to him without tripping over her words?

Ruth shook her head, trying to focus on the task at hand. She picked up a block of beeswax, inhaling its sweet, earthy scent. As she began to melt it down, she allowed herself to daydream, just a little.

In her mind's eye, she saw herself standing behind a booth at the market. But instead of being alone and overwhelmed, Daniel was there beside her.

His presence was comforting, his smile encouraging. Together, they greeted customers and showcased their crafts.

The fantasy was so vivid that Ruth nearly dropped the pot of melted wax. She set it down carefully, her cheeks flushing at the direction her thoughts had taken.

It was silly to imagine such things. Daniel probably saw her as nothing more than his younger sister's shy, wallflower friend. She'd never even spoken to him at a singing.

Still, as Ruth poured the wax into a mold, she couldn't quite shake the image from her mind. Maybe, just maybe, this market could be the start of something new. A chance to step out of her comfort zone and share her passion with others.

As the morning wore on, Ruth found herself humming softly while she worked. It was a hymn her *Mamm* often sang, a song about trusting in *Gott's* plan. The familiar melody soothed her nerves and reinforced her decision.

When the sun had climbed high in the sky, Ruth heard her *Mamm* calling her for lunch. She looked around her workshop, at the dozens of candles she'd created. Each one was a piece of her heart, a testament to her skill and dedication.

"I can do this," she whispered to herself, running her fingers along the smooth surface of a freshly poured candle. "With *Gott's* help, and maybe Daniel's too, I can do this. I will do this," she vowed, with a fierce and determined nod.

Ruth felt a newfound determination while she cleaned up her workspace and prepared to join her family for the midday meal.

Yes, she was still nervous about the market. Yes, the thought of interacting with so many strangers still made her stomach flutter. But for the first time in a long while, Ruth felt like she was standing on the edge of something exciting.

She paused at the door of her workshop, looking back at her creations. A small smile played at the corners of her mouth.

Walking towards the house, Ruth's mind drifted once again to Daniel. She wondered what he would say when Sarah told him about her suggestion.

Would he even be willing to share a booth with someone like her? Or would he prefer to work alone, unburdened by her shyness and inexperience?

Ruth shook her head, trying to dispel the doubts creeping in. She had made her decision, and now she needed to trust in *Gott's* plan.

Whatever happened at the market, she would face it with faith and courage. Even if he didn't want to work with her, she'd at least try it and keep the commitment she'd made to herself.

The scent of her *Mamm's* cooking wafted through the air as Ruth approached the house. For a moment, she hesitated on the porch, her hand on the doorknob.

Should she tell her parents about her decision to participate in the market? They had always been supportive of her candle-making, but they also worried about her shyness and tendency to withdraw from social situations.

Taking a deep breath, Ruth pushed open the door. The warm air of the kitchen enveloped her, along with the comforting smells of home-cooked food. Her *Mamm* looked up from her place beside the stove, a smile spreading across her face.

"There you are, Ruth," she said warmly. "I was beginning to think you'd skip lunch altogether, lost in your candles."

Ruth managed a small smile. "*Nee, Mamm.* I wouldn't miss your cooking."

While helping to set the table, Ruth's mind raced. Should she tell them now? Or wait until she had spoken with Daniel? The weight of her decision seemed to press down on her, making her movements clumsy and distracted.

"Is everything all right, Ruth?" her *Daed* asked, his brow furrowed with concern. "You seem... preoccupied."

Ruth took a deep breath, her fingers finding her apron strings once again. It was now or never. "*Mamm, Daed,*" she began, her voice barely above a whisper. "I... I've decided to participate in the Christmas market."

The kitchen fell silent. Ruth kept her eyes fixed on the floor, afraid to see disappointment or worry on her parents' faces. But when she finally looked up, she was met with expressions of surprise and cautious joy.

"Oh, Ruth," her *Mamm* said, pulling her into a warm embrace. "That's *wunderbar* news. Your candles are so beautiful – they deserve to be shared with the world. And with you there, customers are sure to feel your passion and be even more eager to bring them home."

Her *Daed* nodded in agreement. "We're proud of you, Ruth. It takes courage to step out of your comfort zone."

Ruth felt tears prickling at the corners of her eyes. "*Danki,*" she whispered. "I'm... I'm nervous, but I think it's the right thing to do."

As they sat down to eat, Ruth shared Sarah's suggestion about partnering with Daniel. Her parents exchanged a knowing look that Ruth couldn't decipher, but they seemed supportive of the idea.

"The Fishers are a *gut familye*," her *Daed* said thoughtfully. "And Daniel is a hard worker. I think it could be a fine partnership."

As the meal progressed, Ruth felt a weight lifting from her shoulders. With her parents' support and the possibility of working with Daniel, the market was a little less daunting. She even found herself looking forward to it.

Just a little.

After lunch, Ruth returned to her workshop with a new energy. As she worked on her candles, she allowed herself to imagine what her booth might look like.

Perhaps, as Sarah suggested, Daniel could make some wooden displays for her candles. The thought made her smile.

As the afternoon wore on, Ruth's excitement grew. Although she was still nervous and the thought of interacting with so many strangers still made her stomach flutter, those feelings were tempered with a sense of purpose and possibility.

When the sun began to set, casting long shadows across her workshop, Ruth stepped back to survey her day's work. Dozens of candles stood in neat rows, each one a fine example of her skill and passion. For the first time, she allowed herself to feel truly proud of what she had created.

"I can do this," she whispered to herself, running her fingers along the smooth surface of a freshly poured candle. "With *Gott's* help, and maybe Daniel's too, I *can* do this."

Ruth tidied for the day and went to join her family for supper, more determined than ever.

Yes, she was still anxious about the market. Yes, the thought of working alongside Daniel made her heart race in ways she didn't quite understand. But for the first time in a long while, Ruth felt like she was standing on the edge of something exciting.

She paused at the door of her workshop, looking back at her creations. A small smile played at the corners of her mouth. "Look out, world," she whispered, her voice barely audible. "Ruth Brenneman is coming to the Christmas market."

With that declaration, soft as it was, Ruth stepped out of her workshop and into the crisp December evening. The path ahead was uncertain, but she was ready to take the first step. And who knew, maybe working with Daniel Fisher would turn out to be the best decision she'd ever made.

As she walked towards the house, the cool air nipping at her cheeks, Ruth's mind whirled with possibilities. What would it be like to work alongside Daniel? Would he see her differently once they spent time together? And most importantly, would she be able to overcome her shyness and truly shine at the market?

Only time would tell. But for now, Ruth was content to embrace the nervous excitement bubbling within her. Tomorrow would bring new challenges and opportunities. And for once, Ruth Brenneman was ready to face them head-on.

Chapter 2

D aniel hefted the last crate of wooden crafts onto the rickety table, grinning as he surveyed his handiwork. The Christmas market booth was coming together nicely, even if it was a far cry from the polished displays he'd seen in Lancaster. He'd arrived at dawn, eager to set up before the crowds descended.

"This'll knock their socks off," he muttered, carefully arranging a set of intricately carved nativity figures. His fingers traced the delicate features of the tiny wooden Mary, remembering the hours he'd spent hunched over his workbench, perfecting every detail. He'd worked with an *Englisch* master craftsman during his rumspringa, learning the ins and outs of his chosen craft from an entirely different perspective.

Sometimes, he rather missed the specialized tools the *Englisch* used. But he'd committed to the plain life, and that meant no more electric power tools although he was hopeful to one day convince his community of the wonders of battery-powered tools. Some of the progressive Amish communities used them after all, so it wasn't without precedent. And their community wasn't especially strict compared to others, at least based on what he'd heard from meeting a few Old Order youth on their own rumspringa.

A gentle breeze rustled through the canvas tent, carrying the scent of fresh pine and hot cider. Daniel inhaled deeply, his excitement building. This was his chance to show the community what he could do, to prove that his "modern" ideas weren't a threat but an opportunity.

While he was adjusting a display of wooden ornaments, a timid voice breathed behind him. "*Gut* morning, Daniel."

He turned, his face breaking into a warm smile when he saw Ruth Brenneman standing at the entrance to the booth. She clutched a box of candles to her chest, her eyes darting nervously around the space.

"Ruth! *Gut* morning to you too," Daniel said, moving to help her with her load. "I was wondering when you'd show up. *Kumm* on in, there's plenty of room for both of us."

Ruth hesitated for a moment before stepping inside. "I hope I'm not too late. I... I wasn't sure how early to *kumm*."

Daniel waved off her concern. "*Nee*, you're right on time. Here, let's see where we can set up your candles."

While they worked together to arrange Ruth's creations, Daniel admired the exquisite detail in each one. Delicate snowflakes, lifelike pinecones, and festive holly leaves adorned the surfaces, catching the early morning light.

"These are incredible, Ruth," he said, genuinely impressed. "I've never seen candles like these before."

Ruth's cheeks flushed at the compliment. "*Danki*," she murmured, her fingers fidgeting with her apron strings. "Your woodwork is amazing too. I've always admired it from afar."

Daniel's heart swelled at her words. He'd noticed Ruth at community gatherings before, always quiet and keeping to herself. But now, seeing her artistic talent up close, he realized there was much more to her than met the eye.

"I think our crafts complement each other perfectly," he said, stepping back to admire their combined display. "Just wait until the *Englischer* customers see this. They'll be lining up around the block!"

Ruth's eyes widened. "Do you think there will be very many *Englisch* customers? I thought this was mainly for Amish communities."

Daniel shook his head, his enthusiasm bubbling over. "*Nee*, that's the beauty of it. We can reach so many more people when we open up to *Englischer* visitors. Last year, they outnumbered the Amish visitors, even. And I've actually been thinking about asking around to see if there's an *Englisch* vendor who might partner with me on setting up and running an online store-"

He cut himself off when he saw Ruth's expression turn from curious to concerned. "I mean, not right away, of course. But imagine how many more people could appreciate our crafts if we expanded our reach. And I wouldn't be running the store. Or... or taking pictures for it or anything. Just supplying the products," he finished, feeling a little defensive.

Before Ruth could respond, a gruff voice called out from outside the booth. "Daniel Fisher? Are you in there?"

Daniel recognized the voice of Bishop Stoltzfus and felt a twinge of apprehension. He'd been expecting this conversation, but he'd hoped to have more time to prepare.

"*Jah*, Bishop," he called back, putting on his most respectful smile as the older man entered the booth, followed by two other community leaders. "*Gut* morning. What brings you here so early?"

Bishop Stoltzfus's eyes narrowed as he took in the elaborate display. "We've been hearing some... concerning rumors about your plans for this market, Daniel."

Daniel's smile faltered slightly, but he pressed on. "Oh? What kind of rumors?"

"There's talk of you wanting to partner and sell to the *Englischers*," one of the other elders, Jacob Yoder, chimed in. "And even more worrying, something about computers and the internet."

Daniel took a deep breath, acutely aware of Ruth's presence behind him. He hadn't meant to involve her in this, but now she was witnessing firsthand the conflict he faced.

"With all due respect," Daniel began carefully, "I don't see the harm in welcoming *Englisch* customers. Our crafts are a way to demonstrate our faith and way of life. Sharing them could be a form of witness."

Bishop Stoltzfus's frown deepened. "And the internet? You know our stance on such worldly technologies, Daniel."

Daniel felt a flash of frustration, but he forced himself to remain calm. "I understand your concerns, Bishop. But the world is changing, and if we don't adapt, we risk being left behind. And an online presence doesn't have to compromise our values if we partner with the right person."

The elders exchanged worried glances. "This is precisely what we feared," Jacob Yoder said. "Daniel, you're treading a dangerous path. These modern ideas could lead our young people astray."

Before Daniel could defend himself further, a new voice joined the conversation. "*Gut* morning, everyone. Is there room for one more in this discussion?"

Eli Yoder, Jacob's son and a young man known for his traditional views, stepped into the booth. His eyes lingered on Ruth for a moment before turning to Daniel with a hint of challenge.

"Eli," Daniel nodded, trying to keep the tension from his voice. "What brings you here?"

Eli smiled, but it didn't quite reach his eyes. "Just wanted to see what all the fuss was about. I have to say, Daniel, your work is impressive. But I can't help but wonder if it's too... fancy for our simple way of life."

Daniel bit back a retort, aware of the elders watching closely. "Our craftsmanship is a gift from *Gott*," he said instead. "I believe we honor Him by doing our best work, no matter how simple or elaborate."

Eli nodded, his gaze drifting back to Ruth. "And what do you think, Ruth? Do you agree with Daniel's... progressive ideas?"

All eyes turned to Ruth, who looked like she wanted to disappear into the ground. Daniel felt a surge of protectiveness, wishing he could shield her from this uncomfortable situation.

"I... I think..." Ruth began hesitantly, her voice barely above a whisper. "I think our work speaks for itself. Whether it's traditional or modern, what matters is the heart behind it."

Daniel couldn't help but smile at her words. Even in her shyness, Ruth had managed to cut to the heart of the matter.

The tension in the booth was broken by the arrival of another visitor. Hannah Zook, a quiet young woman from a struggling family, slipped in quietly.

"Oh, I'm sorry," she said, noticing the crowd. "I didn't mean to interrupt."

Daniel's concern immediately shifted as he took in Hannah's appearance. Her dress was worn and patched in several places, and dark circles shadowed her eyes. She looked exhausted and worried, a very different sense from the festive atmosphere of the market.

"*Nee*, you're not interrupting at all," Daniel said warmly, grateful for the distraction. "*Kumm* in, Hannah. How can we help you?"

Hannah's eyes widened as she looked at the display. "Oh, Daniel, your woodwork is beautiful," she breathed. "I... I was wondering if you might need any help setting up or during the market. I could use the work, if there's any available."

Daniel's heart went out to her. He knew the Zook family had fallen on hard times, but he hadn't realized things were this bad.

"Of course, Hannah. We'd be happy to have your help. Why don't you *kumm* back this afternoon, and we'll figure out a schedule?"

Relief washed over Hannah's face. "*Danki*, Daniel. That's very kind of you." She glanced nervously at the elders before adding, "I should go. My *Mamm* needs me at home. But I'll be back later."

As Hannah hurried away, Daniel couldn't shake the feeling that something was deeply wrong. The worry in her eyes, the desperation in her voice... it was a reminder of the real struggles facing their community, beyond debates about tradition and progress.

Mutual aid was one of their values, wasn't it? So, why did she look so distressed, and so fearful about finding work to help her family?

The elders, seeming to sense that the moment had passed, began to make their way out of the booth. Bishop Stoltzfus paused at the entrance, fixing Daniel with a stern look.

"We'll be watching closely, Daniel. Don't forget who you are and where you *kumm* from."

As the group dispersed, leaving Daniel and Ruth alone once more, a heavy silence fell over the booth. Daniel's mind raced, torn between his excitement for the market and the weight of the community's expectations.

Ruth's soft voice broke through his thoughts. "Are you all right, Daniel?"

He turned to her, forcing a smile. "*Jah*, I'm fine. Just... a lot to think about."

Ruth nodded, her eyes full of understanding. "For what it's worth," she said hesitantly, "I think your ideas have merit. Change can be scary, but sometimes it's necessary. Even for us."

Daniel felt a surge of gratitude for her words. "*Danki*, Ruth. That means a lot coming from you."

As they returned to setting up their booth, Daniel's mind kept drifting back to Hannah. What was going on with the Zook family? And did it tie into the larger issues facing their community?

The market hadn't even opened yet, and already Daniel felt like he was standing at a crossroads. His desire to innovate and reach out to the wider world clashed with the pull of tradition and community expectations. And now, with Hannah's situation weighing on his conscience, he realized that the challenges ahead were far more complex than he'd imagined.

As the sun climbed higher in the sky, casting a warm glow over the market grounds, Daniel took a deep breath. Whatever lay ahead, he was determined to face it with faith, compassion, and an open mind. This Christmas market was just the beginning of his dreams.

And he suspected that this season would bring changes no one but *Gott* could see coming.

Chapter 3

R uth's heart pounded as she handed the intricately carved wooden ornament to the smiling customer. Her fingers trembled slightly, but she managed a small smile of her own.

"*Danki* for your purchase," she said softly, her voice barely audible above the market's cheerful bustle.

As the customer walked away, Ruth let out a shaky breath. She'd done it - her first sale of the day. Well, sort of.

No one had bought a candle yet, but Daniel had stepped back, gesturing for her to handle the transaction. She glanced at him now, and he gave her an encouraging nod from his side of their shared booth.

"You're doing great, Ruth," he said warmly. "See? Nothing to be afraid of."

Ruth felt her cheeks warm at his praise. She still couldn't quite believe she was here, surrounded by the sights and sounds of the Amish Christmas market in Bird-in-Hand.

The crisp December air carried the mingled scents of cinnamon, pine, and wood smoke, creating a festive atmosphere that even her anxiety couldn't completely dampen. She breathed in the fresh air, finding it bracing and energizing.

Of course, they had a small propane heater, and she was bundled up. Without that, she'd likely feel much different!

As she arranged a display of her candles, Ruth's mind drifted to the events of the morning. She'd arrived at the market before dawn, her stomach in knots.

Daniel had already been there, setting up their shared booth with an efficiency that both impressed and intimidated her. He'd greeted her with a smile that made her heart skip a beat, and she'd fumbled with her boxes of candles, nearly dropping one in her nervousness.

"Here, let me help," Daniel had said, taking the box from her hands. His fingers had brushed against hers, sending a jolt through her that had nothing to do with the chilly morning air.

Then, the odd confrontation with the bishop and the Yoders... well. She knew from Sarah that Daniel came back from rumspringa with a lot of ideas, but the online store he'd suggested was shocking.

Though, was he really suggesting something so far afield? They already contracted with *Englischers* who ran storefronts selling their goods. Was contracting with one who happened to sell from an online storefront so different?

She was relieved when Hannah's interruption broke the tension. The opening of the market sent her anxiety ratcheting up again.

But now, hours later, Ruth was slowly beginning to relax.

The steady stream of customers kept her busy, and Daniel's presence was a comforting constant. She found herself sneaking glances at him when he wasn't looking, admiring the way his strong hands deftly manipulated the wooden crafts he was selling.

"Excuse me," a voice said, pulling Ruth from her thoughts. She looked up to see a couple standing before her, their bright clothing marking them as *Englisch* visitors with a single glance. The woman's bright earrings sparkled in the sunlight. "These candles are just beautiful! How do you make them?"

Ruth hesitated, her old shyness threatening to overwhelm her. But then she felt Daniel's reassuring presence beside her, and she took a deep breath.

"Well," she began, her voice gaining strength as she spoke, "it starts with selecting the right wax and sometimes, fragrant oils. Then, I carefully blend them together, adding natural dyes for color..."

While Ruth explained her process, she was surprised to find herself genuinely enjoying the interaction. The couple, who introduced themselves as Mike and Linda, seemed fascinated by every detail.

"And you do all this without electricity?" Linda asked, her eyes wide. "That's amazing!"

Ruth nodded, a small smile playing at her lips. "*Jah*, we find ways to create beauty without modern conveniences."

Mike leaned in, his voice dropping to a conspiratorial whisper. "But surely you must use some technology, right? I mean, how else could you make such perfect candles?"

Ruth blinked, taken aback by the question. "*Nee*, we don't use modern technology. It's all done by hand, as our people have done for generations."

Mike and Linda exchanged a look that Ruth couldn't quite decipher. "Well, they're certainly impressive," Linda said, her tone a little too bright. "We'll take three, please."

Ruth wrapped their purchases, unable to shake the feeling that there was something off about the couple's intense curiosity. She glanced at Daniel, who had been quietly observing the interaction.

He raised an eyebrow, silently asking if she was okay. Ruth gave a small nod, grateful for his unspoken support.

The day continued, and Ruth found herself falling into a rhythm. She and Daniel worked seamlessly together, their crafts complementing each other in ways she hadn't anticipated. His wooden candle holders perfectly showcased her scented creations, while her delicate wax ornaments nestled beautifully among his carved figurines.

As the morning wore on, Ruth became aware of a growing undercurrent of tension in the market. She overheard snippets of conversation from neighboring booths, and whispers about small items going missing.

"Did you hear?" an elderly woman at the next booth leaned over to say. "The Yoders' booth had some money stolen right out of their cash box!"

Ruth's eyes widened. "That's terrible," she said, instinctively glancing at their own money box. "Who would do such a thing?"

The woman shrugged. "No one knows. But keep an eye out, *jah*? These *Englisch* visitors... you never know."

As the woman walked away, Ruth felt a pang of guilt. She thought of Mike and Linda, with their overly curious questions. Could they have been casing the booths, looking for easy targets?

But then she shook her head, chastising herself for jumping to conclusions. It wasn't the Amish way to be so suspicious.

"Everything okay?" Daniel asked, noticing her furrowed brow.

Ruth hesitated, then quietly relayed what she'd heard about the thefts. Daniel's expression grew serious.

"That's concerning," he said, his voice low. "We should be extra careful with our cash and valuables."

As they discussed how to better secure their booth, a familiar face appeared. Hannah Zook approached, her eyes darting nervously around the market.

"*Gut* morning, Hannah," Ruth greeted her warmly. "How are you enjoying the market?"

Hannah's smile seemed forced. "Oh, it's... nice," she said distractedly. Her gaze lingered on the cash box for a moment before snapping back to Ruth's face. "I couldn't help overhearing... are there really thieves at the market?"

Daniel nodded grimly. "It seems so. We're trying to figure out how to improve security."

Hannah's eyes lit up with an intensity that surprised Ruth. "Oh! I might have some ideas about that," she said quickly. "My *daed* used to work security at an *Englisch* factory when he was on rumspringa. He taught me a few things."

Hannah launched into a detailed explanation of various security measures, and Ruth found her attention wandering. Something about Hannah's behavior struck her as odd.

The young woman's hands fluttered nervously as she spoke, and there was a desperation in her eyes that Ruth couldn't quite place.

"Here, let me show you," Hannah said suddenly, reaching for one of Ruth's candles. As she picked it up, Ruth noticed her hands were shaking violently.

"Hannah," Ruth said gently, placing a steadying hand on the other woman's arm. "Are you feeling all right?"

Hannah jerked away as if burned, nearly dropping the candle in the process. "I'm fine," she said quickly, her eyes darting around once more. "I just... I need to go. Excuse me. I-I'll be back later, though! T-to discuss the schedule."

As Hannah hurried away, Ruth exchanged a worried glance with Daniel. What was going on with Hannah? And how did it connect to the thefts at the market?

Before Ruth could voice her concerns, another customer approached their booth. She pushed her worries aside, focusing on the task at hand. But as she worked, she couldn't shake the nagging feeling that something was very wrong.

The morning stretched into early afternoon, and the market grew even busier. Ruth found herself gaining confidence with each interaction, surprising herself with how easily she was able to converse with strangers. Daniel's presence was a constant source of comfort and encouragement, and she found herself drawn to his warmth and easy manner.

During a lull in customers, Ruth took a moment to really look at Daniel. He was arranging a display of wooden toys, his strong hands moving with a grace that belied their size. As if sensing her gaze, he looked up and caught her eye, offering a smile that made her heart flutter.

"You're doing wonderfully, Ruth," he said, his voice low and warm. "I knew you had it in you."

Ruth felt her cheeks flush. "*Danki*, Daniel," she murmured. "I couldn't have done this without you."

For a moment, they just looked at each other, and Ruth felt something shift between them. There was a softness in Daniel's eyes that she'd never noticed before, a tenderness that made her breath catch in her throat.

The moment was broken by the arrival of more customers, and Ruth turned away, her mind whirling. What was happening to her? She'd known Daniel for years, and, yes, found him attractive.

But suddenly, he felt like a stranger; a fascinating, attractive stranger who made her pulse race and her palms sweat.

While she helped a young mother choose between two scented candles, Ruth's thoughts kept drifting back to Daniel. She found herself hyper-aware of his presence, of every almost-touch and shared glance. It was exhilarating and worrying all at once.

But even as she grappled with these new feelings, Ruth couldn't shake her concern about the thefts and Hannah's strange behavior. She kept an eye out for Mike and Linda, wondering if her initial suspicions had been unfair. And every time she saw a flash of Hannah's familiar dress in the crowd, she felt a twinge of worry. Was Hannah alright?

As the early afternoon sun filtered through the market's canvas tents, Ruth found herself at a crossroads. She was proud of how far she'd come in just one morning, overcoming her shyness and connecting with customers.

She was excited by the possibilities that seemed to be blossoming between her and Daniel. But she was also troubled by the undercurrent of tension that ran through the market. Not to mention the tension between Daniel, the bishop, and the Yoders. She had a feeling that their conversation was only the beginning.

Ruth took a deep breath, inhaling the mingled scents of her candles and Daniel's woodwork. After today, she knew she was stronger than she'd ever given herself credit for.

With Daniel by her side and her faith to guide her, she felt ready to face whatever the rest of the Christmas Market might bring.

As she turned to greet the next customer, Ruth caught sight of Hannah once more. The young woman was hovering near a booth across the way, her hands fidgeting nervously with her apron strings.

As Ruth watched, Hannah reached out towards a display of handmade quilts, her fingers trembling visibly. She clutched the edge of one, looking heartbroken and terrified.

Ruth's heart rate sped up. What was wrong with Hannah? Was Ruth able to help her?

Certainty settled in her heart. She had to try to help the young woman.

Having found her own strength, Ruth knew it was her responsibility to help others. Watching Hannah let her hand drop away from the quilt and walk off with hunched shoulders and a broken expression, Ruth resolved to start with her. Reaching out to someone was nothing Ruth ever expected to do but reach out she would.

The true test of her newfound strength was yet to come.

Chapter 4

Daniel's hands moved swiftly, wrapping the delicate wooden ornament in tissue paper. "There you go, ma'am," he said, handing the package to the smiling customer. "*Danki* for your purchase. Have a blessed day!"

As the woman walked away, Daniel had to grin. The third day of the Christmas market was in full swing, and their booth was bustling with activity.

He glanced at Ruth, who was explaining the intricacies of her candle-making process to an elderly couple. Her cheeks were flushed with excitement, her eyes bright as she spoke. It warmed his heart to see her coming out of her shell.

"We make a pretty *gut* team, eh?" he said when she finished with the customers.

Ruth's smile was shy but genuine. "*Jah*, we do. I never thought I'd enjoy this so much."

Daniel leaned in, lowering his voice. "You know, Ruth, I've been thinking. With how well we're doing, we could really expand this operation. Maybe even set up that online store for the *Englischers* I mentioned-"

"Daniel Fisher!" a stern voice interrupted. Daniel looked up to see Ruth's parents approaching, their faces a mixture of concern and disapproval.

"Mr. and Mrs. Brenneman," Daniel greeted them, straightening up. "*Gut* morning. How are you enjoying the market?"

Mrs. Brenneman's lips were pressed into a thin line. "We need to speak with you, Daniel. In private."

Daniel's stomach dropped, but he nodded. "Of course. Ruth, can you manage for a few minutes?"

Ruth looked between her parents and Daniel, confusion evident on her face. "*Jah*, I'll be fine."

Daniel followed the Brennemans to a quiet corner of the market, his mind racing. What could they want to discuss?

"Daniel," Mr. Brenneman began, his voice low and serious. "We're concerned about your influence on our Ruth."

"My influence?" Daniel repeated, genuinely confused.

Mrs. Brenneman nodded. "We've heard about your... progressive ideas. The online store, selling to the *Englischers* on the Internet? It's not our way."

"With all due respect," Daniel said, trying to keep his voice calm, "I'm just trying to help our community thrive. The world is changing, and we need to adapt-"

"That's exactly what we're worried about," Mr. Brenneman cut in. He scowled at the younger man. "Ruth is impressionable. She's always been shy, content with our traditional ways. But now, with you encouraging her..."

Daniel felt a flare of frustration. "I'm not trying to change Ruth. I'm just helping her to see her own potential."

Mrs. Brenneman's expression softened slightly. "We know you mean well, Daniel. But you must understand our concerns. We're going to speak with Ruth about this later."

Before Daniel could respond, a commotion from nearby caught their attention. They turned to see a group of vendors gathered around one of the booths, their voices raised in alarm.

"*Another* theft?" Mr. Brenneman muttered, his brow furrowed. "What do they mean by another' one?"

Daniel's heart sank. The thefts continued over the past two days, casting a shadow over the otherwise joyful market.

"Excuse me," he said to the Brennemans. "I should go see what's happening."

As he approached the group, he could hear snippets of conversation.

"...right out of my cash box!"

"...third time this week!"

"...must be one of those *Englisch* visitors..."

Daniel pushed his way to the center of the crowd. "What's going on?" he asked, his voice carrying over the murmurs.

Sarah Hersh, an elderly woman who ran a quilting booth, turned to him with tears in her eyes. "Oh, Daniel! Someone stole the money from my cash box while I was helping a customer. It was only for a moment, but when I turned back, it was gone!"

Daniel's mind raced. This was getting out of hand. "Has anyone called the police?"

A few of the vendors shifted uncomfortably. Involving the *Englisch* authorities wasn't something they did lightly.

"We should handle this ourselves," Jacob Yoder, one of the community elders, spoke up. "We don't need outsiders involved in our affairs."

Daniel took a deep breath. "I understand the hesitation, but this is getting serious. We can't just ignore it and hope it goes away."

He looked around at the worried faces of his friends and neighbors. An idea struck him.

"Well, what if we formed a committee to investigate? We could keep an eye out, talk to people, try to figure out who's behind this ourselves, instead of involving the *Englischers*. The vendors who were robbed are all Amish, after all."

There were murmurs of agreement from the crowd. Daniel felt a surge of pride. This was what he was good at - taking charge and finding solutions.

"I volunteer to lead the committee," he said. "Who else wants to help?"

Several hands went up, including, to Daniel's surprise, Eli Yoder's. Eli was known for his traditional views, and he and Daniel often butted heads. But desperate times called for unlikely alliances, he supposed.

As the crowd began to disperse, Daniel remembered something. "Oh, Elder Jacob," he called out to the elder. "Hannah Zook mentioned she might have some ideas about improving security. Her *daed* used to work security at an *Englisch* factory, apparently. It was years ago when he was on rumspringa, but still."

Jacob's eyebrows shot up. "Hannah Zook?"

Daniel nodded. "*Jah*, that's right. I thought it might be worth hearing her out."

Jacob exchanged glances with the other elders present. "I'm not sure that's wise, Daniel. We don't know anything about *Englischer* security measures. And the Zooks... well, they've had their troubles."

Daniel felt a flare of frustration. "But if she has knowledge that could help us-"

"Daniel," another elder, Samuel Lapp, interrupted. "We appreciate your enthusiasm, but this is exactly the kind of thing we're worried about. These modern ideas, involving the *Englisch* ways... it's not our way."

Daniel bit back a retort at that familiar, tired refrain. But he knew arguing would only make things worse.

"I understand your concerns," he said carefully. "But surely we can at least listen to what Hannah has to say? We don't have to implement anything we're not comfortable with."

The elders exchanged looks again. Finally, Jacob sighed. "We'll consider it. But, Daniel, you need to be careful. Your ideas... they're causing quite a stir in the community. Some are worried you're straying from our ways. That your commitment to our faith is... temporary."

Daniel's breath caught in his lunges. A weight settled in his chest. Temporary?

That was wrong. Utterly, completely wrong.

He opened his mouth to defend himself, but movement at the edge of the crowd caught his eye. Hannah Zook was there, engaged in what looked like an intense conversation with Eli Yoder. Their heads were bent close together, and Hannah's expression was guarded, almost nervous.

As Daniel watched, Hannah glanced around furtively, then slipped something into Eli's hand. Eli quickly pocketed it, nodding gravely.

Daniel's mind raced. What was going on there?

He'd always thought Eli and Hannah barely knew each other. And what had she given him?

"Daniel?" Jacob's voice brought him back to the present. "Did you hear what I said?"

Daniel blinked, tearing his gaze away from Hannah and Eli. "*Jah*, sorry. I understand your concerns. I'll... I'll think about what you've said."

The elders walked away, and Daniel's mind was a whirlwind of thoughts. The thefts, the community's resistance to his ideas, Ruth's parents' disapproval, and now this strange interaction between Hannah and Eli. It was all connected somehow, he was sure of it.

But how?

He made his way back to his booth, where Ruth was waiting with a worried expression.

"Is everything okay?" she asked. "What did my parents want?"

Daniel forced a smile. "Nothing to worry about," he lied, not wanting to burden her. "Just some concerns about the market. How about we focus on our customers for now? Did you make any sales while I was gone?"

"*Jah.*" Ruth nodded but Daniel could see the doubt in her eyes.

As they turned to greet the next customer, he couldn't shake the feeling that things were about to get a lot more complicated. The Christmas market which had started with such promise, was turning into something far more challenging than he'd ever anticipated.

As the day wore on, Daniel found himself constantly scanning the crowd, his mind churning with questions. He noticed Mike and Linda, the overly curious *Englisch* couple, examining various booths with intense interest.

Were they really just enthusiastic visitors, or was there something more to their presence? The market wasn't *that* large, and they'd been back every single day.

"Daniel?" Ruth's soft voice broke through his thoughts. "Are you sure everything's all right? You seem... distracted."

He turned to her, seeing the concern in her warm brown eyes. For a moment, he was tempted to confide in her, to share the weight of his worries.

But then he remembered her parents' words, their fear of his influence on her. He swallowed hard.

"I'm fine, Ruth," he said, forcing a smile. "Just thinking about some new designs for my woodwork. How about you? Are you enjoying the market so far?"

Ruth's face lit up, and Daniel felt a pang in his chest. She looked so happy, so alive. How could her parents think he was a bad influence?

"Oh, Daniel, it's wonderful!" she exclaimed. "I never thought I'd enjoy talking to strangers so much. But it's only one-on-one, which isn't so bad. And seeing people appreciate my candles... it's a dream *kumm* true."

Daniel's smile became genuine. "I'm so glad, Ruth. You deserve this success. Your work is truly beautiful."

A blush crept up Ruth's cheeks, and she ducked her head shyly. "*Danki*, Daniel. I couldn't have done it without you. Without your support."

For a moment, they just looked at each other, and Daniel felt something shift between them. There was a softness in Ruth's eyes that he'd never noticed before, a warmth that made his heart race.

The moment was broken by the arrival of more customers, and they turned back to their work. But Daniel found his gaze continually drawn to Ruth throughout the afternoon.

He watched as she confidently explained her candle-making process, her hands moving gracefully as she demonstrated different techniques.

As the day progressed, Daniel's pride in their partnership grew. Despite the challenges they faced, he and Ruth were a formidable team. Their crafts complemented each other perfectly, and customers often commented on how well their booth was arranged.

During a lull in customers, Daniel decided to broach the subject of expansion again.

"Ruth," he said, his voice low and excited, "I've been thinking. With how well we're doing, we could really take this to the next level."

Ruth looked at him curiously. "What do you mean?"

Daniel leaned in, his eyes sparkling with enthusiasm. "Well, what if we didn't just sell at markets? We could set up a small shop in town, maybe even reach out to some of the *Englisch* stores in Lancaster. And with the Internet-"

He cut himself off, remembering the elders' warnings. But to his surprise, Ruth didn't look shocked or scandalized. Instead, her eyes were wide with interest, if a little guarded.

"Go on," she urged, curious. "You mentioned that before... what about the Internet?"

Daniel hesitated, then decided to throw caution to the wind. "We could set up an online store, if we find the right *Englisch* partners. It would allow us to reach customers all over the country, maybe even the world. Just imagine, Ruth; your candles could be burning in different homes across the country. In New York, California, maybe even Europe!"

Ruth's expression was a mixture of excitement and uncertainty. "But... is that allowed? What would the elders say?"

Daniel sighed, running a hand through his hair. "That's the tricky part. They're... not exactly thrilled with some of my ideas. But, Ruth, I truly believe this could be amazing for our community. We could bring in more money; create more jobs. We wouldn't have to change who we are or compromise our values. We'd just be... adapting."

Ruth was quiet for a moment, her brow furrowed in thought. Finally, she spoke. "It sounds wonderful, Daniel. But also a little scary. I'm not sure I'm ready for something so... big."

Daniel nodded, trying to hide his disappointment. "I understand. It's just an idea for now. We don't have to decide anything right away."

They returned to their work and Daniel couldn't help but feel a twinge of frustration. He knew his ideas could help the community if only they'd give them a chance.

But between the elders' skepticism, Ruth's parents' disapproval, and now, facing Ruth's hesitations after letting her curiosity lift his hopes, he was beginning to feel very alone in his vision.

The afternoon wore on, and the market began to wind down for the day. As Daniel and Ruth started to pack up their booth, he noticed Hannah Zook hovering nearby, looking nervous.

"Hannah?" he called out. "Is everything okay? It's not time to help us break down the stall for another few hours, yet."

She approached hesitantly, her eyes darting around. "Daniel, I... I was wondering if you'd spoken to the elders about my security ideas?"

Daniel nodded. "I mentioned it to them. They seemed ... hesitant, but they said they'd consider it."

Hannah's face fell. "Oh. I see."

"Don't worry," Daniel reassured her. "I'll keep pushing for it. Your ideas could really help with the theft problem."

Hannah's eyes widened at the mention of the thefts. "Right. The thefts. I... I should go. I-I'm sorry, I can't help with things after the market tonight. My *mamm* needs me at home."

Daniel couldn't shake the feeling that something was off as she hurried away. He remembered the secretive exchange he'd witnessed between Hannah and Eli earlier.

What was going on?

Just then, he spotted Eli across the market. The other young man was watching Hannah's retreating figure with an unreadable expression. As if sensing Daniel's gaze, Eli turned, and their eyes met.

For a moment, there was a flicker of... something in Eli's eyes. Anger? Guilt? Fear?

But then it was gone, replaced by his usual stoic demeanor.

Daniel's mind was racing. Just *what* in the world was going on?

As he and Ruth finished packing up their booth, Daniel felt the weight of the day's events settling on his shoulders. The market had been a success in many ways, but the undercurrent of tension and suspicion was impossible to ignore.

"Daniel?" Ruth's voice broke through his thoughts. "Are you sure you're okay? You've seemed worried all afternoon."

He looked at her, taking in her concerned expression, the way the fading sunlight caught the golden strands in her hair. In that moment, he wanted nothing more than to confide in her, to share the burden of his worries and doubts.

But then he remembered her parents' words, their fear of his influence. And he thought of the elders' warnings, the community's growing unease with his ideas.

He couldn't drag Ruth into this, not when she was just coming out of her shell and finding her confidence.

"I'm fine, Ruth," he said, forcing a smile. "Just tired from a busy day. You did amazing, you know. I'm really proud of you."

Ruth's face lit up at his praise, and Daniel felt a mixture of warmth and guilt wash over him. As they said their goodbyes and headed home for the evening, he couldn't shake the feeling that he was standing at a crossroads.

On one side was the path of tradition, of playing it safe and keeping the peace. On the other was the road of progress, of pushing boundaries and fighting for what he believed in.

And somewhere in the middle was Ruth, her growing confidence and blossoming talent, a beautiful example of what could happen when tradition and progress found a way to coexist.

Daniel hitched up his horse for the ride home, his mind a whirlwind of questions. What was the connection between Hannah and Eli? Who was behind the thefts?

And most importantly, how could he navigate these choppy waters without losing sight of what truly mattered - his faith, his community, and the growing bond between him and Ruth?

The Christmas market had started as a simple opportunity for business. Now, it felt like the catalyst for something much bigger, a turning point not just for Daniel but for the entire community.

As he urged his horse forward, Daniel sent up a silent prayer. Whatever challenges lay ahead, he would face them with faith, determination, and the hope that somehow he could find a way to bridge the gap between the old ways and the new.

Chapter 5

The scent of her *Mamm's* freshly baked bread filled the kitchen, but not even that comforting aroma could quell the anxiety bubbling in Ruth's chest. Her parents' concerned gazes weighed heavily upon her, their words echoing in her mind. Ruth's fingers trembled as she smoothed the wrinkles from her apron, not meeting their eyes.

"Ruth," her *Daed* began, his voice gentle but firm. "We're worried about you spending so much time with Daniel Fisher at the market. His ideas... they're not our way."

Ruth's heart sank. She'd known this conversation was coming, but that didn't make it any easier.

"But Daed," she protested softly, "Daniel's just trying to help our community. His woodwork complements my candles so well, and-"

"We know, *liebling*," her *Mamm* interrupted, reaching out to pat Ruth's hand. "But Daniel's talk of online stores and selling to the *Englischers* all across the world... it's causing quite a stir. We don't want you to get caught up in all that. I-I know that Daniel is a handsome young *mann*, and quite charming... and you're of the age where such things can turn your head, but, Ruth, I don't think he's a *gut* choice."

Ruth bit her lip, fighting back tears. How could she explain the way Daniel made her feel?

How his encouragement had helped her overcome her shyness? How her heart fluttered every time she saw his smile?

"Have you considered Eli Yoder?" her *Daed* asked, his tone hopeful. "He's a *gut* young *mann*, traditional. He'd make a fine husband."

Ruth's cheeks flushed. "Eli? But I hardly know him."

"That's what courtship is for, dear," her *Mamm* said gently. "Give him a chance. He's been asking about you. Nothing official, but still."

Ruth nodded mutely, her mind whirling. As she prepared to leave for the market, her parents' words echoed in her ears.

Eli Yoder. Traditional. A fine husband.

But all she could think about was Daniel's warm laugh and the way his eyes lit up when he talked about his ideas for the future. The way he was so sure they could build something wonderful together.

The market was already bustling when Ruth arrived. She made her way to their booth, her heart skipping a beat when she saw Daniel arranging his wooden crafts. He looked up as she approached, his face breaking into a wide smile.

"*Gut* morning, Ruth!" he called out cheerfully. "Ready for another busy day?"

Ruth managed a small smile in return. "*Jah*, I think so," she said softly, setting down her box of candles.

As they worked side by side, Ruth couldn't help but notice how easily Daniel interacted with the customers.

His warm demeanor and quick wit drew people in, and more than once, she found herself captivated by the sound of his laughter.

"You're doing great," Daniel said during a lull, giving her an encouraging smile. "Your candles are flying off the shelves."

Ruth felt her cheeks warm at his praise. "*Danki*, Daniel. It's all thanks to your help."

Just then, a familiar figure approached their booth. Eli Yoder, tall and handsome in his traditional Amish attire, smiled shyly at Ruth.

"*Gut* morning, Ruth," he said, his voice soft. "Your candles look beautiful today."

Ruth felt a flutter of... something in her chest. Was it attraction? Or just nervousness?

"*Danki*, Eli," she replied, acutely aware of Daniel watching their interaction. "How are you enjoying the market?"

As Eli chatted about his family's booth, Ruth found her gaze drifting back to Daniel. He was helping a customer, but she could see the tension in his shoulders.

Was he... jealous?

The thought both thrilled and terrified her. She liked Daniel - more than she should, perhaps. Certainly, more than her parents would like to hear.

Her parents' words rang in her ears. Eli was the safe choice, the one her family would approve of. The one they *already* approved of.

Daniel... Daniel was a risk.

As the afternoon wore on, Ruth's inner turmoil grew. She found herself drawn to Daniel's warmth and enthusiasm, even as she tried to give Eli's soft-spoken kindness a chance. It was as if her heart and her head were at war, and she didn't know which side to choose.

The *Englisch* couple, Mike and Linda, returned to their booth late in the day. Their enthusiasm seemed forced this time, and Ruth noticed them asking pointed questions about their setup and security measures.

"So, do you leave your cash box here overnight?" Mike asked, his eyes darting around the booth.

Daniel shook his head. "*Nee*, we take everything of value home each night."

Linda leaned in, her voice lowered. "Smart. We've heard there've been some... incidents at the market. Thefts, you know? It's a shame, a lovely little market like this facing such unseemly challenges."

Ruth and Daniel exchanged a worried glance. The rumors of theft had been circulating for days but hearing it from outsiders made it feel more real, somehow.

After Mike and Linda moved on, Ruth couldn't shake a feeling of unease. She watched as they lingered near a jewelry booth, their heads bent close together in whispered conversation. Were they really just innocent shoppers, or was there something more sinister at play?

The market was winding down for the day when Daniel turned to Ruth with a hesitant smile. "So, are you going to the Sunday singing tomorrow?" he asked, his voice casual but his eyes hopeful.

Ruth's heart skipped a beat. "*Jah*, I am," she replied, trying to keep her voice steady. "Are you?"

Daniel nodded. "I thought maybe we could walk there together? If you'd like, that is."

Ruth knew she should say no. Her parents' warnings echoed in her mind. But looking into Daniel's warm eyes, she found herself nodding.

"I'd like that," she said softly. "I can meet you at the end of the lane to my *haus*?"

He nodded, grinning brightly as the sun and wide as the cloudless blue sky above.

She smiled back, helplessly drawn to him.

The next evening, while they walked to the singing together, Ruth felt a mix of excitement and guilt. Daniel's presence beside her was comforting, and she found herself opening up to him in a way she never had before.

"I've always loved music," she confided as they neared the meeting house. "Sometimes, when I'm making candles, I hum hymns to myself. It helps me focus."

Daniel's face lit up. "That's beautiful, Ruth. You should sing a solo sometime."

Ruth laughed, shaking her head. "Oh, *nee*. I could never. I'm not that *gut*."

"I bet you are," Daniel said softly, his hand brushing against hers. The touch sent a jolt through Ruth, and she quickly pulled away, her cheeks burning.

Inside the meeting house, Ruth found herself hyper-aware of Daniel's presence. His voice, rich and deep, blended beautifully with the others as they sang familiar hymns. More than once, she caught herself watching him instead of following along in her hymnal.

As the evening progressed, Ruth noticed Hannah Zook slip out early, her face pinched with worry. A few minutes later, she overheard two women whispering near the back of the room.

"Did you hear about the Zooks?" one said, her voice low. "They're in real financial trouble. I heard they might lose the farm."

The other woman clucked her tongue sympathetically. "Such a shame. And with Hannah's *Mamm* being so ill..."

Ruth's brow furrowed. She'd known Hannah's family was struggling, but she hadn't realized it was this bad. And what did this have to do with Hannah's strange behavior at the market?

As the singing came to an end, Ruth found herself more conflicted than ever. Her growing feelings for Daniel warred with her desire to please her family. The mystery surrounding Hannah and the market thefts added another layer of complexity to an already confusing situation.

Walking home with Daniel, Ruth mulled over everything she'd learned. She wanted to confide in him, to share her worries and seek his advice. But something held her back.

Was it fear? Loyalty to her family? Or something else entirely?

"Ruth?" Daniel's voice broke through her thoughts. They had stopped in front of the turn-off to her family's *haus*, the warm glow of lamplight spilling from the windows visible even at this distance. "Is everything alright? You seem... distracted."

Ruth looked up into his concerned face, her heart aching with unspoken words. "I'm fine," she lied, forcing a smile. "Just tired from the long day."

Daniel nodded, but she could see the doubt in his eyes. "Well, if you ever need to talk..." he trailed off, leaving the offer hanging in the air between them.

"*Danki*, Daniel," Ruth said softly. "*Gut* night."

As she watched him walk away, Ruth felt a wave of longing wash over her. She wanted to call him back, to pour out her heart and ask for his help in unraveling the mysteries piling up around them.

But instead, she turned and walked into her home, where she knew her parents were waiting. As she closed the door behind her, Ruth couldn't shake the feeling that she was closing the door on more than just the night.

She was at a crossroads, and the path she chose would shape more than just her own future.

With a heavy heart, Ruth prepared for bed, her mind whirling with unanswered questions. What was really going on with Hannah and her family? Who was behind the market thefts?

And most importantly, how could she reconcile her growing feelings for Daniel with her family's expectations?

As she drifted off to sleep, Ruth's last thoughts were of Daniel's warm smile and the way his hand felt brushing against hers. Before she fell asleep, one last thought crossed her mind: her heart was no longer entirely her own.

Chapter 6

D aniel's fist clenched around the piece of paper in his hand, his jaw set in determination as he faced the group of community elders. The late afternoon sun filtered through the windows of the meeting house, casting long shadows across the room.

"With all due respect," Daniel said, struggling to keep his voice level, "I believe these expansion ideas could bring real benefits to our community. An online store would allow us to reach customers far beyond Bird-in-Hand."

Bishop Stoltzfus shook his head, his brow furrowed in disapproval. "Daniel, we've discussed this before. Our ways have served us well for generations. We don't need to change them now."

Daniel took a deep breath, trying to quell his rising frustration. "But think of the opportunities, Bishop. We could create more jobs, bring in more income for our families. We can do this, without having to compromise our values--"

"Enough," Elder Yoder interrupted, his voice sharp. "This talk of computers and Internet sales... it's *not our way*, Daniel. You're treading a dangerous path. Stop walking down it, before it's too late."

The other elders nodded in agreement, their faces showing a mixture of concern and disappointment. Daniel felt his heart sink. He'd hoped that by presenting his ideas formally, he might be able to sway them. But it seemed his efforts had only deepened their resolve.

"I understand your concerns," Daniel said, desperate. He had to keep trying. At least one last time. "But the world is changing. If we don't adapt, we risk being left behind."

Bishop Stoltzfus stood, signaling the end of the discussion. "We appreciate your enthusiasm, Daniel. But our decision is final. No online stores, no expansion beyond our traditional markets. That's the end of it."

As the elders filed out of the room, Daniel remained rooted to the spot, his mind whirling. How could they not see the potential? The good they could do for their community?

With a heavy sigh, he made his way out of the meeting house and back to the Christmas market. The festive atmosphere felt at odds with his tumultuous emotions. Vendors called out cheerfully to passersby, the air filled with the scent of cinnamon and woodsmoke and pine boughs, freshly woven into wreaths with cheerful red holly berries peeking out from the needles.

Daniel spotted Ruth at their shared booth, carefully arranging a display of candles. The sight of her brought a small smile to his face, despite his frustration. He made his way over, his steps heavy.

"How did it go?" Ruth asked as he approached, her eyes searching his face.

Daniel shook his head, leaning against the booth. "Not well. They won't even consider it, Ruth. They think I'm trying to change our entire way of life."

Ruth's expression softened with sympathy. She reached out, her hand hovering lightly above his arm for a beat before she pulled it back without touching him. He was disappointed she hadn't let her hand rest on his arm, even for half a second. But that was ridiculous. Of course, she hadn't.

Ruth was a *gut* woman, faithful and true to their ways.

Unlike Daniel, at least according to the elders.

"I'm sorry, Daniel. I know how much this meant to you," she said.

Her almost touch still sent a warmth through him, easing some of the tension in his shoulders.

"I just don't understand," he said, his voice low. "Can't they see I'm trying to help our community? To create opportunities for our young people?"

Ruth nodded, her brow furrowed in thought. "Maybe they're just scared of change. It's a big step, going from our traditional ways to selling online, even using a third party to run it."

Daniel sighed, running a hand through his hair. "I know. But we wouldn't have to change who we are. We'd just be... expanding our reach."

For a moment, they stood in companionable silence, watching the bustle of the market around them. Then Ruth's face lit up with an idea.

"You know," she said, a hint of excitement in her voice, "maybe we can't expand online right now. But what if we tried something new here at the market?"

Daniel raised an eyebrow, intrigued. "What do you mean?"

Ruth's eyes sparkled as she explained, "Well, we've been working side by side, but what if we combined our skills? Your woodworking and my candle-making. We could create something unique, something that showcases both our talents."

As Ruth spoke, Daniel felt a spark of hope ignite in his chest. He nodded eagerly, his mind already racing with possibilities. "That's brilliant, Ruth! We could make custom-sized wooden candle holders, or maybe decorative boxes with scented wax inlays..."

For the next hour, they huddled together, sketching ideas and discussing techniques. Daniel marveled at how easily they worked together, their skills complementing each other perfectly. As they talked, he found his earlier frustration fading, replaced by a renewed sense of purpose.

"Ruth," he said softly, catching her eye. "Thank you. I was feeling pretty low after that meeting, but this... this has given me hope."

Ruth's cheeks flushed pink, but her smile was warm. "That's what friends are for, Daniel. We'll figure this out together."

Just as they were putting the finishing touches on their designs, a commotion from nearby caught their attention. Sarah Hersh, the elderly vendor who sold quilts, was in tears, surrounded by a group of concerned marketgoers.

Daniel and Ruth exchanged worried glances before hurrying over. "What happened?" Daniel asked, his voice laced with concern.

Sarah looked up, her face streaked with tears. "My cash box," she said, her voice trembling. "It's gone. I-I sold three quilts. All of today's earnings, just... vanished."

A murmur rippled through the crowd. Daniel felt his stomach drop. This wasn't the first theft at the market, but it was certainly the boldest. To steal an entire cash box in broad daylight...

"We need to do something," he said, his voice carrying over the worried whispers. "This can't go on. We need better security measures."

Several people nodded in agreement, but others looked skeptical. "What kind of measures?" someone asked.

Daniel hesitated for a moment, knowing his next words might be controversial. But the image of Sarah's tearful face steeled his resolve.

"I think we should consider installing security cameras," he said firmly. "They could act as a deterrent and help us catch the thief if it happens again. They make battery-powered ones that run on a loop and don't need other devices to check."

The reaction was immediate and mixed. Some vendors nodded eagerly, while others looked shocked at the suggestion. Ruth's eyes widened, and she tugged gently on Daniel's sleeve.

"Are you sure about this?" she whispered. "The elders..."

But Daniel's mind was made up. "I know it's not our usual way," he said, addressing the crowd. "But these thefts are hurting our community. We need to take action."

Before anyone could respond, Bishop Stoltzfus pushed his way through the crowd, his face thunderous. "Daniel Fisher," he said, his voice low and dangerous. His gaze narrowed, as he glared at the young man. "A word. Now."

Daniel's heart sank, but he squared his shoulders and followed the bishop to a quiet corner of the market. He could feel the eyes of the community on him, a mixture of curiosity and concern.

"What do you think you're doing?" Bishop Stoltzfus demanded once they were alone. "Security cameras? It's clear you've lost your way, but have you lost your mind as well?"

Daniel took a deep breath, trying to keep his voice steady. "Bishop, I know it's unconventional. But these thefts are getting worse. We need to protect our people."

The bishop's frown deepened. "And you think embracing worldly technology is the answer? Daniel, I'm deeply disappointed. We just finished discussing the dangers of straying from our ways."

"But this is different," Daniel argued. "This isn't about expanding our business. It's about keeping our community safe."

Bishop Stoltzfus shook his head. "You're not seeing clearly, Daniel. This is a slippery slope. Today it's cameras, tomorrow it's cell phones and computers. Where does it end?"

Daniel felt his frustration rising again. "It ends when our people are safe and prosperous. Isn't that what we all want?"

The bishop's expression softened slightly, but his voice remained firm. "Of course it is. But not at the cost of our values, our way of life. I'm sorry, Daniel, but I can't allow this. No cameras. We'll find another way to deal with the thefts."

As the Bishop walked away, Daniel felt a mixture of anger and defeat wash over him. He'd acted hastily, he knew that now. But the thought of more people like poor Sarah Hersh suffering such devastating losses... it was too much to bear.

He made his way back to the booth, where Ruth was waiting anxiously. "Daniel?" she said softly. "Are you okay?"

He shook his head, unable to meet her eyes. "I messed up, Ruth. I should have thought it through before suggesting the cameras. Now the bishop thinks I'm trying to undermine our entire way of life."

Ruth reached out, this time resting her hand on his arm for a fleeting second. "You were just trying to help," she said gently. "Your heart was in the right place."

Daniel smiled at her gratefully, drawing strength from her unwavering support. As they stood there, a familiar figure approached the booth. Eli Yoder, looking uncharacteristically nervous, cleared his throat to get their attention.

"Daniel," Eli said, his voice low. "Can I talk to you for a moment? In private?"

Surprised by the request, Daniel nodded. He followed Eli to a quiet corner of the market, curiosity mingling with his lingering frustration.

"What's going on, Eli?" he asked once they were alone.

Eli shifted uncomfortably, his eyes darting around as if to ensure they weren't being overheard. "It's about Hannah," he said finally. "Hannah Zook. I... I think she might know something about the thefts."

Daniel's eyebrows shot up in surprise. "Hannah? But she's always been so quiet, so... helpful. What makes you think she's involved?"

Eli sighed heavily. "It's not that I think she's the thief," he explained. "But I overheard her talking to her *daed* the other day. Their *familye* is in real trouble, Daniel. Hannah's *mamm* is very sick, and they can't afford the medical bills. She gave me a paper with an overview of everything, to see if I could do anything. But her *daed* refuses to ask for help."

He scowled. "Or accept it when offered freely."

Daniel felt his heart sink. He'd known the Zooks were struggling, but he hadn't realized things were this bad.

"That's terrible," he said softly. "But what does this have to do with the thefts?"

Eli hesitated, then continued, "I think Hannah might know who's behind it. She seemed... nervous when I asked her about the market. And I've seen her talking to some *Englisch* visitors who've been asking a lot of questions."

Daniel's mind raced, trying to connect the dots. Were Hannah's family troubles and the market thefts related somehow? And what about those *Englisch* visitors? Could they be involved?

"Thank you for telling me this, Eli," Daniel said finally. "I'll keep an eye out, see if I can figure out what's going on."

As Eli walked away, a surge of determination shot through Daniel's veins. He might not be able to implement modern security measures or expand their business online, but he could still help his community. He would get to the bottom of these thefts, one way or another.

Making his way back to the booth, Daniel's mind whirled with possibilities. He caught sight of Ruth, her face illuminated by the soft glow of her candles as she chatted with a customer. The sight of her brought a small smile to his face, despite the weight of everything he'd learned.

As the market began to wind down for the day, Daniel found himself reflecting on the tumultuous events. His expansion ideas had been firmly rejected, his hasty words about the cameras backfired horribly, and now he was faced with a potential connection between the thefts and Hannah's family troubles.

It was a lot to process, but as he helped Ruth pack up their booth, Daniel was reinvigorated. He might have stumbled today, but he wasn't giving up. There had to be a way to help his community, whether or not he ever helped to bridge the gap between tradition and progress.

As they finished closing up, Ruth turned to him, her eyes soft with concern. "Are you going to be okay, Daniel?" she asked quietly.

He nodded, offering her a small smile. "I will be," he said. "It's been a tough day, but... I'm not giving up. There's still so much good we can do here."

Ruth's answering smile was a balm to his troubled soul. "I'm glad to hear that," she said. "And remember, you're not alone in this. We'll figure it out together."

As they parted ways for the evening, Daniel couldn't shake the feeling that he was standing on the brink of something big. The market thefts, Hannah's problems, his own desires for progress... it all felt connected.

Somehow. And he was determined to unravel the mystery, no matter what it took.

With a final glance at the now-quiet market, Daniel headed home, his mind already racing with plans for tomorrow. One way or another, he would find a way to help his community.

And maybe, just maybe, he'd find a way to make his dreams of progress a reality too.

Chapter 7

Ruth fisted the cloth of her apron in both hands, wrinkling the fabric. Her heart pounded so loudly she was sure everyone in the community meeting hall could hear it.

The usually soothing scents of wood polish and peppermint tea did little to calm her nerves as she scanned the room, taking in the sea of familiar faces. Her gaze landed on Daniel, who offered her an encouraging smile from across the aisle. She managed a weak smile in return, grateful for his ever-present support.

As Bishop Stoltzfus called the meeting to order, Ruth took a deep breath, trying to gather her courage. She had practiced her words all afternoon, determined to contribute to the discussion about the recent thefts at the Christmas market. But now, faced with the expectant gazes of her friends and neighbors, she felt her resolve wavering.

"As you all know," Bishop Stoltzfus began, his deep voice carrying easily through the hall, "we've had a series of unfortunate incidents at the Christmas market. Several vendors have reported missing items and cash. We're here tonight to discuss how we can address this problem and ensure the safety of our community."

Ruth's fingers found the edge of her apron, twisting the fabric nervously. She knew she should speak up and share her ideas about increasing security without compromising their values. But the words stuck in her throat, refusing to come out.

"Does anyone have any suggestions?" the bishop asked, his eyes sweeping the room.

Ruth's heart raced. This was her chance. She took a deep breath and slowly raised her hand, willing it not to shake.

"*Jah*, Ruth?" Bishop Stoltzfus nodded in her direction, his expression encouraging.

Ruth stood, her legs feeling like jelly beneath her. "I... I think..." she began, her voice barely above a whisper. She cleared her throat and tried again. "We could... maybe..."

But the words wouldn't come. Ruth felt her cheeks burning as the silence stretched on, the weight of everyone's stares pressing down on her. She could hear whispers starting to ripple through the crowd, and her embarrassment threatened to overwhelm her.

"I'm sorry," she mumbled, sinking back into her seat, wishing the floor would open up and swallow her whole.

Just as the bishop was about to move on, Daniel's voice rang out clear and strong. "Ruth has some excellent ideas," he said, standing up. "If I may, I'd like to share the first few of them on her behalf, if that's all right?" he asked, tilting his head as he met her frustrated gaze.

She nodded, once, in a rough, jerking movement. What was he going to say?

Ruth's eyes widened in surprise as Daniel began to outline the very suggestions she'd practiced all afternoon. He spoke of organizing volunteer patrols, creating a buddy system for vendors, and even suggested discreetly marking valuable items to make them easier to track if stolen.

As Daniel spoke, Ruth was grateful, even as frustration washed over her. She was thankful for his support, but completely disappointed in herself for not being able to voice her own ideas.

The community's reaction to Daniel's words was mixed. Some nodded in agreement, while others looked skeptical. Ruth noticed Eli Yoder leaning forward, his expression thoughtful as he listened to Daniel's words.

"These are interesting suggestions," Bishop Stoltzfus said when Daniel finished. He glanced at her with a furrowed brow. "But some of them seem... unconventional. We must be careful not to stray too far from our ways in our efforts to solve this problem."

Ruth's heart sank at the bishop's words, but she couldn't deny the truth in them. As much as she wanted to embrace new ideas, she knew the importance of respecting their traditions.

As the meeting continued, Ruth found herself retreating into her thoughts. She might not have been able to speak up, but that didn't mean she couldn't contribute. There had to be another way she could help, something that would blend their traditions with the need for progress.

When the meeting finally adjourned, Ruth slipped out quietly, her mind already racing with new ideas. She headed straight for home. For her workshop.

Ruth couldn't face anyone right now, not Daniel, not Sarah, and not her parents.

She barely noticed the cold night air curling around her in small gusts or the crunch of newly fallen snow beneath her feet. Ruth focused on her breathing, fighting to steady her inhales and exhales.

Once inside the familiar space, surrounded by the comforting scents of beeswax and herbs, Ruth's anxiety began to ebb at last. She moved to her worktable, her hands already reaching for her supplies.

For the next hour, Ruth lost herself in her craft. Her fingers moved deftly, blending traditional techniques with new ideas.

She infused her special blend of oils into the wax, creating a unique scent that spoke of home and safety. As she worked, she poured her hopes and fears into the candle, imbuing it with a sense of purpose.

When she finally stepped back to admire her creation, Ruth felt a small spark of pride. The candle was beautiful, its surface adorned with intricate carvings that told a story of community and protection. It was a perfect blend of old and new, just like the solution they needed for their current troubles.

A soft knock at the door startled her from her thoughts. "*Kumm* in," she called, her voice steadier than it had been all evening.

Daniel stepped into the workshop, his eyes widening as he took in the candle on her worktable. "Ruth, this is beautiful," he said, moving closer to examine it. "What inspired this?"

Ruth felt her cheeks warm at his praise. "I wanted to create something that represented our community," she explained softly. "Something that showed we can embrace new ideas while still honoring our traditions."

Daniel nodded, his expression thoughtful. "It's perfect," he said. "Just like your ideas at the meeting. I'm sorry if I overstepped by sharing them. I just couldn't bear to see you struggle like that."

Ruth shook her head, offering him a small smile. "*Nee*, don't apologize. I'm grateful for your help. I just wish..." she trailed off, her fingers finding her apron strings.

"You'll find your voice, Ruth," Daniel said gently. "At the market, you already have. So, I know you will here, too.

And when you do, the whole community will benefit from your wisdom."

His words warmed her heart, and Ruth found herself believing them if only a little. "*Danki*, Daniel," she said softly. "For everything."

They stood in comfortable silence for a moment, the candle flickering between them. Then Daniel seemed to remember something.

"Oh, I almost forgot. I wanted to talk to you about organizing those volunteer patrols we discussed at the meeting. I think if we can get enough people involved, we might be able to deter the thief."

Ruth nodded eagerly, grateful for the chance to contribute. "That's a wonderful idea. We could create a schedule to make sure every booth is covered throughout the day."

As they began to discuss the logistics, another knock sounded at the door. This time, it was Eli Yoder who entered, his tall frame filling the doorway.

"I hope I'm not interrupting," he said, his eyes moving between Ruth and Daniel. "I was just walking Hannah home and saw the light on. I overheard you talking about volunteer patrols. I'd like to help, if you'll have me."

Ruth smiled warmly at Eli, touched by his offer. "Of course, Eli. We'd be grateful for your help."

She couldn't help but notice the subtle tension that seemed to crackle between Eli and Daniel as they exchanged stiff nods. It made her uncomfortable, though she couldn't quite put her finger on why.

"*Gut*," Eli said, his gaze lingering on Ruth. "Just let me know what you need."

As they continued to discuss their plans, Ruth's mind drifted to Hannah Zook. She'd noticed the young woman at the meeting, looking pale and worried. An idea began to form in Ruth's mind.

"Excuse me for a moment," she said to Daniel and Eli. "There's something I need to do."

Ruth made her way across the yard to where Hannah was standing by the fence, staring out into the distance with a forlorn look on her tired face.

"Hannah," she called out softly. "Please, do you have a moment?"

Hannah turned, her eyes widening in surprise. "Ruth? Is everything all right?"

Ruth nodded, offering a gentle smile. "*Jah*, I just... I wanted to see how you were doing. I heard your *Mamm* hasn't been feeling well."

Hannah's expression softened, though Ruth couldn't help but notice a guarded look in her eyes. "That's very kind of you, Ruth. *Mamm*... she's struggling, but we're managing."

"I made this for her," Ruth said, pulling a small jar from her apron pocket. "It's a special blend of herbs and beeswax. She can rub it on her chest, and it can help soothe any coughing."

Hannah hesitated for a moment before taking the jar, her fingers trembling slightly. "*Danki*, Ruth. This is... very thoughtful of you."

As Hannah tucked the jar into her pocket, Ruth couldn't shake the feeling that there was more going on than met the eye. Hannah's nervous energy, the way her eyes darted around... it all seemed so unlike the quiet, composed young woman Ruth recalled from their schoolgirl days in years past.

"Hannah," Ruth said gently, "if there's anything else you need, anything at all, please don't hesitate to ask. I'm here for you. We're all here for you."

For a moment, something flashed in Hannah's eyes - gratitude? Fear? - but it was gone so quickly Ruth wasn't sure she'd seen it at all.

"*Danki*," Hannah said again, her voice barely above a whisper. "I... I really should go. *Mamm* will be wondering where I am."

As Hannah hurried away, Ruth frowned. What was she missing?

It felt important. She turned to head back to her workshop, her mind whirling with questions.

Just then, a snippet of conversation she'd heard but not registered from earlier crossed her mind, almost like she was hearing it again in her ear right now. She closed her eyes, traveling back to the market.

She recognized the voices of Mike and Linda, the *Englischer* couple who had been asking so many questions at the market.

"...incredible value," Mike was saying, his voice low but excited. "These Amish crafts could fetch a fortune in the right market."

"Shh," Linda hushed him. "Not here. We'll discuss it later."

Ruth froze, her eyes closed, heart pounding. What were they talking about? And why did it sound so... suspicious?

As Mike and Linda's footsteps faded away in her memory, replaced by a customer asking about her candles, Ruth opened her eyes.

In the darkness, she stood rooted to the spot, her mind racing. The thefts, Hannah's strange behavior, and now this newly recalled conversation...

Could it all be connected somehow? It must be, right?

She prayed *Gott* would lead her to the answers and carry them all through the rest of the Christmas season with His strength.

With a shaky breath, Ruth turned back towards her workshop, where both Daniel and Eli were waiting. The mystery surrounding their peaceful community was far from solved.

And somehow, she knew she had to play a part in unraveling it - whether she was ready for that role or not.

Chapter 8

"..and as we reflect on the story of Joseph, let us consider how his integrity in the face of temptation strengthened not only his own faith but also the bonds of his community," Daniel concluded, his deep voice resonating through the cozy living room of his family's farmhouse.

The small group gathered for Bible study nodded in agreement, their faces illuminated by the warm glow of oil lamps. Daniel felt a sense of peace wash over him as he looked around at his friends and neighbors. This was what community was all about: coming together, sharing wisdom, and supporting one another.

When the group began to disperse, exchanging quiet goodnights and bundling up against the chilly December air, Daniel was lost in thought. The story of Joseph always resonated with him, but tonight it felt particularly poignant. Like Joseph, he often felt caught between two worlds – the traditional Amish way of life he'd been raised in, and the pull toward progress and innovation he felt in his heart.

"That was a wonderful lesson, Daniel," Ruth's soft voice broke through his reverie. He looked up to see her standing by the doorway, her warm brown eyes meeting his. "I especially liked what you said about integrity being the foundation of a strong community."

Daniel felt his heart skip a beat. "*Danki*, Ruth," he said, offering her a smile. "I'm glad it resonated with you."

After the last of the guests filed out, Daniel and Ruth found themselves alone in the living room. The silence between them was comfortable, filled with unspoken understanding.

"So," Ruth began, her fingers fidgeting with her apron strings, "Have you given any more thought to those market security measures we discussed?"

Daniel nodded, his expression turning serious. "*Jah*, I have. I think I've found a compromise that might work."

He led Ruth to the kitchen table, where he'd laid out some sketches and notes. "I know the elders weren't keen on the idea of security cameras," he explained, "but what if we used battery-powered alarms instead? I also considered pressure-plate alarms that are mechanical, not electric, and we could set those up discreetly under cash boxes. Or, we can add bells inside the lids, so any time the box opens, it rings. Then, the battery-powered alarms for different items, or on a display case when a vendor is pulled away."

Ruth leaned in, studying the drawings with interest. "That's clever, Daniel," she said, a note of admiration in her voice. "It's a *gut* balance between modern security and our traditional values."

Daniel felt a surge of pride at her words. This was why he valued Ruth's opinion so much – she understood his desire to innovate while still respecting their way of life.

"I think it could work," he said, his excitement growing. "We'd need to get approval from the elders, of course, but I believe they'll see the merit in this approach."

Ruth nodded, but Daniel noticed a flicker of hesitation in her eyes. "What is it?" he asked gently. "You don't think it's a *gut* idea?"

"*Nee*, it's not that," Ruth said quickly. "It's just... well, I've been thinking. What if the thief isn't an outsider? What if it's someone from our own community?"

Daniel felt a chill run down his spine. The thought had crossed his mind, but hearing Ruth voice it made it feel more real somehow. "You think one of our own would do such a thing?" he asked, his voice low.

Ruth shrugged, looking uncomfortable. "I hope not but... well, desperation can drive people to do things they normally wouldn't. Maybe instead of focusing so much on catching the thief, we should be looking for ways to help those who might be struggling."

Daniel frowned, considering her words. "I see your point," he said slowly, "but we can't just ignore the thefts. People are losing money, Ruth. Their livelihoods are at stake."

"I know," Ruth sighed. "I just think we need to approach this with compassion as well as caution."

Their discussion was interrupted by the arrival of Daniel's younger sister, Sarah. "Daniel," she called from the doorway, "*Daed* wants to speak with you."

Daniel nodded, exchanging a glance with Ruth. "We'll continue this later," he said softly. "Meet me at the market tomorrow morning?"

Ruth agreed, and Daniel watched her leave, his heart heavy with the weight of their conversation. As he made his way to his father's study, the continued thefts weighed on his heart. Was Ruth right? Could it be someone from their own community?

His father, John Fisher, was sitting at his desk when Daniel entered. "Sit down, *Sohn*," he said, gesturing to a chair. "We need to talk."

Daniel took a seat, bracing himself for what was to come. His father had been increasingly concerned about his "progressive" ideas lately.

"I overhear your conversation with Ruth," John began, his voice carefully neutral. "You're planning to propose different kinds of alarms to add at the market? Including electronic ones?"

Daniel nodded, straightening in his chair. "*Jah, Daed.* I believe it's a *gut* compromise between security and our values."

John sighed, rubbing his forehead. "Daniel, I understand your desire to help, but you must be careful. These modern ideas... they're causing quite a stir in the community."

"But, *Daed*," Daniel protested, "we can't just ignore the problem. The thefts are hurting our people."

"I know, *Sohn*," John said gently. "But there are other ways to address this issue. Ways that don't involve bringing worldly technology into our midst."

Daniel felt a flare of frustration, but he fought to keep his voice calm. "What would you suggest, then?"

His father leaned back in his chair, considering. "Your previous suggestions had merit. We could organize more volunteer patrols. And the bells, while they might become intrusive, could deter the thief."

Daniel nodded, seeing the wisdom in these suggestions. "Those are *gut* ideas, *Daed*. But I still think the alarms could be useful. They're not so different from the battery-powered flashlights we already use sometimes."

John's expression softened slightly. "I know you mean well, Daniel. Just... tread carefully, *jah*? And speaking of treading carefully," he added, his tone changing, "I've noticed you spending a lot of time with Ruth Brenneman lately."

Daniel felt his cheeks warm. "Ruth is a *gut* friend," he said carefully. "We work well together at the market."

His father's eyes twinkled knowingly. "Just a friend, eh? Well, she's a fine young woman. But, Daniel," he continued, his voice growing serious, "you should know that some in the community are concerned. They worry that Ruth's more traditional ways might... clash with your tendencies. Hold you back, in a way."

Daniel bristled at this. "Hold me back? Ruth understands me better than anyone, *Daed*. She supports my ideas, even if she doesn't always agree with them."

John held up his hands in a placating gesture. "I'm just telling you what I've heard, *Sohn*. You know I only want what's best for you."

Daniel nodded, feeling a mixture of gratitude and frustration. "I know, *Daed. Danki* for your concern."

Leaving his father's study, Daniel's mind was whirling. He appreciated his father's advice, but he was frustrated. Why was the community so quick to judge both his ideas and his relationship with Ruth? Weren't they supposed to leave judgment to *Gott* alone?

The next morning dawned crisp and clear, the December sun casting long shadows across the snow-covered landscape. Daniel arrived at the Christmas market early, eager to set up his booth and implement some of the new security measures he'd discussed with Ruth.

As he worked, he saw Eli Yoder watching Ruth from across the market. The sight sent a jolt of jealousy through him, for which he immediately felt guilty.

Ruth was free to talk to whomever she wanted, and Eli was a *gut mann*. Still, Daniel couldn't deny the way his stomach clenched when he saw Eli approach Ruth, a shy smile on his face. He turned away, busying himself with the booth set-up.

"*Gut* morning, Daniel," a voice called, pulling him from his thoughts a few minutes later. He turned to see Eli approaching, his expression friendly.

"*Gut* morning, Eli," Daniel replied, forcing a smile. "How can I help you?"

Eli glanced around before lowering his voice. "I heard you're working on some new security measures for the market. I was wondering if you could use an extra pair of hands?"

Daniel blinked in surprise. He hadn't expected Eli, known for his strict adherence to all things tradition, to be interested in his plans.

"That's... that's very kind of you, Eli," he said cautiously. "What did you have in mind?"

Eli began to share his ideas and Daniel found himself warming to the other man. Despite their differences, Eli was genuinely concerned about the community's welfare. They spent the next hour discussing various strategies, from increased patrols to subtle ways of marking valuable items.

As their conversation drew to a close, Eli's expression grew serious. "There's something else you should know, Daniel," he said, his voice low. "It's about Hannah Zook and her *familye*."

Daniel leaned in, his interest piqued. He'd noticed Hannah's strange behavior lately but hadn't been able to piece together what was wrong.

"Hannah's *mamm* is very ill," Eli explained. "The medical bills are piling up, and they're struggling to make ends meet. I've heard rumors that they might lose their farm if things don't improve soon."

Daniel felt a wave of sympathy wash over him. "That's terrible," he said softly. "Is there anything we can do to help?"

Eli shook his head. "Hannah's *daed* is too proud to accept help. He says they don't need charity. But, Daniel..." he hesitated, looking uncomfortable. "I've seen Hannah talking to those *Englisch* visitors who've been asking so many questions. The ones some folks suspect might be involved in the thefts."

Daniel's eyes widened as the implications of Eli's words sank in. Was Hannah connected to the market thefts? Surely that was impossible – Hannah helped them, offered suggestions for improving security...

She was always such a quiet, well-behaved young woman. But if her family was truly in dire straits...

"Thank you for telling me this, Eli," Daniel said, his mind racing. "I'll keep an eye out, see if I can figure out what's going on."

Eli walked away and Daniel found himself lost in thought. The market thefts, Hannah's family troubles, his own desires for progress... it all jumbled together in his thoughts, more tangled than a ball of yarn under the paws of a barn kitten. And at the center of it all was Ruth, her quiet strength and unwavering faith a beacon in the storm of uncertainty.

Daniel looked over to Ruth arranging her candles, her face illuminated by the soft glow of the morning sun. He felt a surge of affection, mixed with a fierce determination. Whatever challenges lay ahead, he would face them with integrity and compassion. And maybe, just maybe, with Ruth by his side.

As the market began to come to life around him, Daniel sent up a silent prayer. *Gott, guide me,* he thought. *Help me find a way to protect our community without losing sight of what truly matters. And please, if it's Your will, help everyone see that our differences don't have to divide us – they might just be the very thing that makes us stronger together.*

With renewed purpose, Daniel turned back to his booth, ready to face whatever the day might bring. Little did he know, the revelations about Hannah's family were just the beginning of a mystery that would test not only his faith but the very foundations of their tight-knit Amish community.

Chapter 9

Daniel's fist clenched around the piece of paper in his hand, his jaw set as he faced the group of community elders. The late afternoon sun filtered through the windows of the meeting house, casting long shadows across the room.

"With all due respect," Daniel said, struggling to keep his voice level, "I believe these new security measures could bring real benefits to our community. The bell system and marked items can very likely help deter potential thefts."

Bishop Stoltzfus shook his head, his brow furrowed in disapproval. "Daniel, we've discussed this before. Our ways have served us well for generations. We don't need to change them now."

Daniel took a deep breath, trying to quell his rising frustration. "But think of the opportunities, Bishop. We could create a safer environment for our vendors, bring in more income for our families. We wouldn't have to compromise our values--"

"Enough," Elder Yoder interrupted, his voice sharp. "This talk of modern security measures... it's not our way, Daniel. You're treading a dangerous path."

The other elders nodded in agreement, their faces a mixture of concern and disappointment. Daniel felt his heart sink. He'd hoped that by presenting his ideas formally, he might be able to sway them. But it seemed his efforts had only deepened their resolve.

"I understand your concerns," Daniel said, trying one last time. "But the world is changing. If we don't adapt, we risk losing everything we've worked for at this market."

Bishop Stoltzfus stood, signaling the end of the discussion. "We appreciate your enthusiasm, Daniel. But our decision is final. No more changes to our security measures. That's the end of it."

As the elders filed out of the room, Daniel remained rooted to the spot, his mind whirling. How could they not see the potential? The good they could do for their community?

Movement from the corner of his eye and a soft presence at his side pulled him from his thoughts. He turned to see Ruth standing beside him, her warm brown eyes filled with concern and support.

"Are you okay?" she asked softly.

Daniel managed a small smile, grateful for her presence. "*Jah*, I'm fine. Just... frustrated."

Ruth nodded, understanding in her gaze. "I know. But don't give up, Daniel. Your ideas are gut. We'll find a way to make them work."

Her words warmed his heart, easing some of the tension in his shoulders. "*Danki*, Ruth. I don't know what I'd do without you."

They made their way out of the meeting house and back towards the Christmas market. As they walked, a new idea began to form in Daniel's mind. He turned to Ruth, his eyes lighting up.

"What if we try a different approach?" he said. "Instead of relying on technology or outside help, we could use our community's strength to catch the thief."

Ruth looked intrigued. "What do you mean?"

"A community watch," Daniel explained, his excitement growing. "We could organize shifts, have people patrolling the market in pairs. Everyone would be involved, keeping an eye out for suspicious activity."

Ruth nodded slowly, considering the idea. "That could work. It's more in line with our traditional values, too. The elders might be more open to it."

Daniel felt a surge of hope. "Exactly. And it would bring the community together, give everyone a sense of ownership in solving this problem."

As they reached the market, Daniel spotted Eli Yoder arranging his display of handmade furniture. To his surprise, Eli waved them over, a friendly smile on his face.

"Daniel, Ruth," Eli greeted them. "How did the meeting with the elders go?"

Daniel sighed, shaking his head. "Not well. They're not open to any new security measures."

Eli's brow furrowed. "That's a shame. We need to do something about these thefts."

Seizing the opportunity, Daniel shared his new idea for a community watch. To his surprise and Ruth's delight, Eli's face lit up with enthusiasm.

"That's brilliant, Daniel," Eli said. "It's a perfect solution. Traditional, community-focused, and effective. I'd be happy to help organize it."

Daniel blinked, momentarily taken aback by Eli's support. He'd always thought of Eli as more traditional, often at odds with his progressive ideas.

Then again, maybe he wasn't giving Eli enough credit. Here he was, offering his help.

"*Danki*, Eli," Daniel said warmly. "That would be a *gut* help."

As they discussed the logistics of the community watch, more vendors gathered around, drawn by their animated conversation. Soon, a small crowd formed, all eager to hear about the new plan.

Daniel felt a surge of confidence as he explained his idea to the group. He could see the nods of approval, the thoughtful expressions as people considered how they could contribute. Even some of the more skeptical community members seemed interested.

"This could really work," Sarah Hersh said. "It's a *gut* way to keep our traditions while addressing the problem."

As the discussion continued, Daniel noticed Hannah Zook hovering on the outskirts of the group. She seemed nervous, her eyes darting around as if looking for an escape. When their gazes met, Hannah quickly looked away, turning to busy herself with her booth.

Daniel frowned, a nagging suspicion tugging at the back of his mind. Hannah had been acting strangely for days now, always on edge. He made a mental note to keep a closer eye on her.

With the community's tentative approval secured, Daniel felt a weight lift from his shoulders. They had a plan, one that respected their traditions while addressing the very real threat to their livelihoods. Now, they just needed to implement it.

As the market began to wind down for the evening, Daniel set about implementing the first steps of their new community watch plan. He assigned pairs of vendors to take shifts patrolling the market, making sure everyone understood their responsibilities.

"Remember," he said to each group, "we're not looking to trap anyone or lure them into acting. This is about prevention. Your presence alone should be enough to deter any potential thief. But we *will* keep an eye out, and if you see something, then speak up."

As he worked, Daniel couldn't shake the nagging worry about Hannah and her family. He kept an eye out for her, but she seemed to have disappeared after the meeting.

Just as he finished closing up his own booth for the night, Ruth having left early for the day, Daniel spotted Hannah hurrying towards the exit. Without thinking, he followed her, his curiosity getting the better of him.

Hannah walked quickly, her head down and her arms wrapped tightly around herself. She didn't seem to notice Daniel following at a discreet distance. As they left the market behind, Hannah took a path that led away from the main road, toward the outskirts of their community.

Daniel's frown deepened as he realized where they were headed. This was the way to the Zook family farm. But why would Hannah be in such a furtive hurry to go home? Usually, she stayed late at the market to help others with closing their stalls, for the extra income.

And why did she look so nervous?

As they crested a small hill, the Zook farmhouse came into view. Daniel's heart sank at the sight. The once-proud home looked run-down, its paint peeling and its roof in desperate need of repair. The fences, usually meticulously tended, stood in disrepair, unkempt and overgrown.

Hannah disappeared inside the house, leaving Daniel at the edge of the property, his mind whirling with questions.

How had things deteriorated so much for the Zooks without anyone noticing? And more importantly, what desperate measures might they be driven to in order to save their home?

As Daniel turned to head back to the market, the front door opened, and two figures stepped out onto the porch. He saw Hannah's father, Joseph Zook, engaged in what looked like an intense conversation with someone Daniel didn't recognize. The stranger was dressed in *Englisch* clothes, a sharp suit accessorized by a watch, light glinting off the metal as he gestured, animated, as he spoke.

Daniel walked in a wide arc, and, sure enough, a shiny car was parked out of sight from the road, on the other side of the barn.

Daniel felt his stomach drop. What was an *Englisch* businessman doing at the Zook farm at this hour? And why did Joseph look so distressed?

As he made his way back to the market, Daniel's mind raced with possibilities. The thefts, Hannah's strange behavior, her family's financial troubles, and now this mysterious *Englisch* visitor... it all had to be connected somehow. But how?

One thing was certain: the situation was far more complex than he had initially thought. As he reached the now-quiet market, Daniel sent up a silent prayer.

Gott, guide me, he thought. *Help me find a way to protect our community without compromising our values. And please, if it's Your will, show me how to help the Zooks before it's too late.*

With new determination, Daniel headed home, his mind already formulating a plan. Tomorrow, he decided he would talk to Hannah. One way or another, he would get to the bottom of this mystery and find a way to help his community – all of his community – before it was too late.

Chapter 10

Ruth's heart pounded as she scanned the bustling Christmas market, her eyes darting from booth to booth. The festive atmosphere felt at odds with the tension coiled in her stomach. Was today the day they would catch the thief who had been plaguing their community?

Daniel's plan didn't involve actively seeking out the thief, but the buddy system was in place and all eyes were eagle-sharp on the lookout for anything suspicious. She took a deep breath, inhaling the mingled scents of cinnamon, pine, and freshly baked bread.

"Everything's in place," Daniel murmured, appearing at her side. His presence was reassuring, a steady anchor in the storm of her nerves. "The community watch is on high alert. If anyone tries anything, we'll catch them."

Ruth nodded, fidgeting with her apron strings. "I hope so," she whispered. "I can't bear the thought of anyone else losing their hard-earned money, especially so close to Christmas."

Daniel's hand found hers, giving it a gentle squeeze. "Have faith, Ruth. We'll get through this together."

As they made their way through the market, Ruth couldn't help but marvel at how seamlessly their plan had come together. Volunteers from the community were strategically positioned throughout the area, their watchful eyes hidden behind the guise of casual browsing. Even Eli Yoder, who had initially been skeptical of their methods, was now fully on board, patrolling the far end of the market.

The hours ticked by, each moment ratcheting up Ruth's anxiety. She tried to focus on her candles, explaining their unique scents and designs to curious customers, but her mind kept wandering.

Every sudden movement, every raised voice sent a jolt through her. Was this it? Had they caught the thief?

Just as Ruth was beginning to wonder if their plan had failed, a commotion erupted near the quilt booth. She exchanged a quick glance with Daniel before hurrying over, her heart in her throat.

"She tried to steal my wallet!" an *Englisch* woman was shouting, pointing accusingly at a young Amish girl who couldn't have been more than fourteen.

Ruth frowned. The girl was Esther Hersh, Sarah's granddaughter.

Her family only arrived the week before to visit for Christmas. *She* couldn't be the thief.

With tears streaming down her face, the teenager vehemently shook her head. "*Nee*, I didn't! I was just looking at the quilts, I swear!"

Ruth stepped forward, her voice steadier than she felt. "Please, let's all calm down," she said, looking between the two. "What exactly happened here?"

The *Englisch* woman, her face red with anger, launched into an explanation. "I was admiring this beautiful quilt when I felt someone bump into me. When I turned around, I saw her hand in my purse!"

The Amish girl sobbed harder. "It's not true! I tripped and fell against her. I never touched her purse!"

Ruth took a deep breath, willing herself to remain calm. She could feel the eyes of the gathered crowd upon her, waiting to see how she would handle this.

"Ma'am," she said to the aggrieved woman, "are you sure you saw her hand in your purse? Could it have been a misunderstanding?"

The woman hesitated, her anger seeming to deflate slightly. "Well... I suppose I didn't actually see her hand in my purse. But I felt the bump, and when I turned around, she was right there!"

Ruth nodded, then turned to the young girl. "And you're certain you just tripped?"

"*Jah*," the girl hiccupped. "I'm so sorry, I didn't mean to cause trouble. I just wanted to look at the quilts. My *grossmammi* is teaching me, and I was hoping to get some ideas."

Ruth sighed. This wasn't their thief – just an unfortunate misunderstanding. She turned back to the *Englisch* woman with a gentle smile.

"I believe there's been a mistake," she said. "Why don't we check your purse? I'm sure everything is still there."

The woman rummaged through her bag, her face reddening for a different reason now. "Oh... oh my. Everything's here. I'm so sorry, I jumped to conclusions."

Ruth nodded, then addressed the crowd. "Let this be a lesson to us all," she said, her voice carrying clearly. "In times of stress, it's easy to let fear and suspicion cloud our judgment. But we must remember to approach each other with kindness and understanding, especially during this holy season."

As the crowd dispersed, murmuring in agreement, Ruth felt a surge of pride. She'd managed to defuse a potentially explosive situation without losing her voice or her composure. Daniel appeared at her side, his eyes shining with admiration.

"That was incredible, Ruth," he said softly. "You handled that perfectly."

Ruth felt her cheeks warm at his praise. "I just did what needed to be done," she murmured.

Their moment was interrupted by the arrival of Mike and Linda, the *Englisch* couple who had been under suspicion for days.

"Excuse us," Mike said, his jovial voice carrying a hint of nervousness. "We couldn't help but overhear what happened. We wanted to clear the air about something."

Ruth and Daniel exchanged glances before turning their attention to the couple. "What is it?" Daniel asked, his voice carefully neutral.

Linda stepped forward, wringing her hands. "We know we've been asking a lot of questions about your crafts and security measures," she began. "And we realize now how suspicious that must have seemed."

Mike nodded, adding, "The truth is, we're not thieves. We're... well, we're dealers, in antiques and fine crafts. We were looking to add in Amish-made, and we were hoping to find some unique pieces for our shop back in Philadelphia."

Ruth blinked in surprise. "Oh! Why didn't you just say so?"

Linda looked sheepish. "We were worried you might not want to sell to us if you knew we were planning to resell the items at a markup. We should have been upfront from the beginning. We're so sorry for any trouble we've caused."

Daniel's posture relaxed slightly. "We appreciate your honesty," he said. "In the future, it's always better to be straightforward. Our community values honesty above all else."

Mike grinned, slinging an arm around Linda's shoulders. "You hear that, Bonnie? We should've come clean from the start."

Linda rolled her eyes good-naturedly. "Oh, hush, Clyde. We're lucky they're being so understanding."

Ruth couldn't help but smile at their playful banter. "Well, now that we've cleared things up, perhaps we could discuss some potential purchases? I'm sure we can come to an arrangement that benefits everyone."

As they began to negotiate, Ruth felt relief settle on her shoulders with Mike and Linda cleared of suspicion, though they were no closer to solving the mystery of the market thefts.

And perhaps this was a good compromise for Daniel's dream of reaching customers across the world. Maybe Mike and Linda even had an online store...

The minutes wore on, and Ruth found herself relaxing into the festive atmosphere. The air was filled with the sound of carols and children's laughter, and the scent of fresh-baked treats wafted through the market.

Perhaps the thief was gone. Maybe he or she didn't want to spoil the market spirit. It was almost Christmas, after all.

Chapter 11

O n the day before Christmas Eve, Ruth's hands were steady as she handed the well-wrapped, intricately carved candle to the beaming customer.

"*Danki* for your purchase," she said softly, with an appreciative smile. "I hope it brings warmth and light to your home this Christmas Season. Have a blessed day."

The *Englisch* woman walked away, cradling the candle like a precious treasure, and Ruth felt a surge of pride. Her special creation, featuring traditional Amish craftsmanship and natural designs meant to appeal to *Englischers*, were flying off the shelves all day.

She'd lost count of how many she'd sold, but the stack of bills in her cash box was growing impressively thick while the stock dwindled ever lower. A fine problem to have, really.

"You're doing amazing, Ruth," Daniel's warm voice came from behind her. She turned to see him grinning, his eyes twinkling with admiration. "I think you've found your niche with these new candles. Especially for next year's market"

Ruth felt her cheeks flush, both from the praise and from Daniel's proximity. "*Danki*, Daniel," she murmured. "I couldn't have done it without your encouragement."

He shook his head, still smiling. "*Nee*, this is all you, Ruth. You've always had this talent inside you. I'm just glad you're finally letting it shine."

Their moment was interrupted by the arrival of more customers, and Ruth turned back to her work. As she explained the unique features of her candles to an interested couple, she caught sight of her parents watching from across the market. Her *Mamm's* expression was a mixture of pride and concern, while her *Daed's* brow was furrowed with what looked like disapproval.

Ruth swallowed hard, pushing down the anxiety that threatened to bubble up. She knew her parents were worried about her growing closeness to Daniel and her increasingly "modern" ideas. But surely, they could see how happy and fulfilled she had been since starting the market?

As the afternoon wore on, Ruth even called out to customers, cajoling them over to her stall to look at her candles and Daniel's goods as well. Then, after the rush of the day was over, Daniel made his way over to her side.

"Ruth," he said, ducking his head and speaking in a low tone. "Can we talk? Somewhere private?"

Ruth's heart skipped a beat, but she nodded. She asked their neighbor to watch the stall, and he nodded amiably.

Then, they slipped away from the bustling market, finding a quiet spot behind one of the storage sheds. The late afternoon sun cast long shadows across the ground, and a chilly breeze rustled through the bare branches overhead.

"What is it, Daniel?" Ruth asked, suddenly nervous. Had she been too forward with her ideas? Was he going to tell her to be more careful, more traditional, to avoid the scrutiny he faced?

But Daniel's eyes were warm as he gazed at her.

"Ruth," he began, his voice low and earnest. "I... I can't stop thinking about you. About us. The way we work together, the way you understand me like no one else does. I think... I think we could have a real future together."

Ruth's breath caught in her throat. "Daniel," she whispered, her heart pounding. He should be speaking to her parents, first. But... she knew why he hadn't.

Why he couldn't right now. They'd only refuse, despite Ruth's feelings, despite everything Daniel had done for her and all the ways he'd helped her find her confidence.

She swallowed, looking up at him with a disbelieving, dawning smile of happiness. "I... I feel the same way. But what about our families? The community? They don't approve of your progressive ideas, and now I'm starting to have them too..."

Daniel reached for her gloved hand, squeezing gently. Her breath hitched. Ruth wished the fabric between them would vanish.

"We'll face it together," he said firmly. "I believe in us, Ruth. In what we could build together. Your creativity, my vision for the future... we could do amazing things."

Tears pricked at the corners of her eyes. She'd never dared to hope for this, never imagined someone could understand and appreciate her the way Daniel did.

"I want that too," she admitted. "But I'm scared, Daniel. What if we're making a mistake?"

He pulled her close, wrapping his arms around her in a warm embrace. "Trust in *Gott*," he murmured into her hair. "He brought us together for a reason. We'll find a way to make it work."

She clung to him, leaning against his chest, taking courage from his strength. As they stood there, holding each other, Ruth relaxed, peace washing over her. Whatever lay ahead, she could face it, move over and through and past any obstacles, with Daniel by her side.

Their moment was shattered by a commotion from the market. They broke apart, exchanging worried glances before hurrying back to see what was happening.

A crowd had gathered around Sarah Hersh's booth. The elderly woman was in tears, her hands shaking as she gestured to her empty display.

"It's gone," she wailed. "My best quilt, the one I've been working on all year. Someone's stolen it! And only two days before Christmas!"

Ruth felt her stomach drop. How had an entire quilt gone missing? There must be more than one culprit.

A sick feeling crawled up her spine. Despite the new security measures, despite the community watch idea, there was yet another theft. The worst one, yet.

She scanned the crowd frantically, looking for any sign of... well, anything. Mike and Linda left earlier, waving their goodbyes with bags full of purchases.

They'd vowed to keep an eye out for the thief while they were still at the market. She'd seen them load their van and leave over an hour earlier.

As the community rallied around Sarah, offering comfort and promises to find the culprit, doubt swept through Ruth.

Who could have taken Sarah's quilt? The thief must have grabbed it and ran, knowing such an audacious theft would be swiftly discovered.

She caught sight of Hannah Zook on the outskirts of the crowd, her face pale and drawn. For a moment, their eyes met, and Ruth saw something flicker in Hannah's expression.

Fear? Guilt? Before she could process it, Hannah had turned away, disappearing into the throng of people.

Daniel appeared at Ruth's side, his face grim. "This is getting out of hand," he murmured. "We need to do something more drastic."

Ruth nodded, her mind racing. But as she looked around at the worried faces of her friends and neighbors, she felt a creeping sense of uncertainty. Her newfound confidence wavered in the face of this latest setback.

What did she know about any of this? Only weeks before, Ruth could hardly speak to a stranger, let alone try and catch a thief!

As the sun set, casting a golden glow over the market, Ruth was paralyzed, facing down a crossroads she never expected.

On one hand, she felt more alive and purposeful than ever before. Her candles were a success, she was finding her voice, and she and Daniel were on the cusp of something beautiful.

But on the other hand, the problems at the market were mounting. The thefts continued despite their best efforts, and it was only a matter of time before their stall was hit.

And even now, she could feel the disapproving gazes of the more traditional community members. Her parents' worried looks from earlier weighed heavily on her heart.

As she began to pack up the booth for the night, hands and feet sluggish and heavy, Ruth's mind whirled with questions.

Had she been too hasty in embracing these new ideas? Was her blossoming relationship with Daniel clouding her judgment? And now, knowing that Mike and Linda weren't behind the thefts, she was back to square one.

A group of *Englisch* teenagers walked by, rowdy and energetic. Her eyes narrowed at one tall young man, distinct with his bright copper hair.

She scanned the rest of the group, too. She'd seen a few of them more than once.

Who was the thief? Was it more than one person?

She carefully wrapped her few remaining candles, each one demonstrating her blossoming creativity and embrace of a new design. As she worked, she caught sight of Daniel across the market, deep in conversation with the elders. His brow was furrowed in concentration, his hands moving animatedly as he spoke.

Ruth's heart swelled with affection, even as a tendril of worry curled in her stomach. She believed in Daniel, in his vision for their community. They hadn't mentioned the idea of the online store again, but she knew it remained one of his goals.

But at what cost would that vision come?

As she closed up her cash box, Ruth's fingers brushed against the stack of bills inside. Her candles were a resounding success with customers, proof that blending tradition and innovation could work. Mere money though... wasn't enough to convince the skeptics.

The market was nearly empty now, most vendors having packed up and headed home. Ruth lingered, her eyes drawn to Sarah Hersh's booth.

The elderly woman was still there, being comforted by her granddaughter and a group of vendors. The sight of her tear-stained face sent a pang through Ruth's heart.

She approached slowly, clutching one of her special candles. "Mrs. Hersh?" she said softly. "I... I wanted you to have this. I know it can't replace your quilt, but I hope it brings you some comfort."

Sarah looked up, her eyes red-rimmed but grateful. "Oh, Ruth," she said, accepting the candle. "That's very kind of you. Your *Mamm* and *Daed* must be so proud of the young woman you're becoming."

Ruth felt a lump form in her throat. Were her parents proud? Or were they worried about the path she was choosing?

As she made her way back to her own booth, Ruth saw Hannah Zook again. The young woman was hurrying away, her head down and her arms wrapped tightly around herself. Ruth frowned, a nagging suspicion tugging at the back of her mind. There was something about Hannah's behavior that didn't sit right with her.

"Ruth?" Daniel's voice broke through her thoughts. He'd finished his conversation with the elders and was now standing beside her, concern etched on his handsome face. "Are you all right?"

She managed a small smile, but it didn't quite reach her eyes. "I'm not sure," she admitted. "Daniel, I... I'm starting to wonder if we're doing the right thing. Maybe we're moving too fast, changing too much."

Daniel's expression softened. He reached out as if to tuck a stray strand of hair behind her ear, but Ruth shied away. What if someone saw?

His expression dropped, turning somber. "Change isn't easy," he said softly. "But that doesn't mean it's wrong. We're trying to help our community, Ruth. To make things better for everyone."

Ruth nodded, glancing around before reaching for his hand behind the counter. She squeezed his fingers lightly, then let go.

"I know," she whispered. "But what if we're wrong? What if we're making things worse?"

Before Daniel could respond, a shout rang out from across the market. They turned to see Eli Yoder running towards them, his face pale with shock.

"Daniel! Ruth!" he called, skidding to a stop in front of them. "You need to come quickly. It's... it's Hannah Zook. She's been caught trying to steal from the donation box for Sarah's quilt fund."

Ruth felt as if the ground had dropped out from beneath her feet. Hannah? The quiet, haunted girl who worked so hard to help her family? How could this be possible?

As they hurried towards the commotion, Ruth's mind raced. She'd been so sure that Mike and Linda were behind the thefts. And when they proved otherwise, she immediately jumped to consider other *Englisch* visitors.

Had her judgment been so clouded by prejudice against the *Englisch* that she'd missed what was happening right under her nose?

The scene that greeted them was chaotic. Hannah was sobbing, standing defeated between two grim-faced vendors.

"Hannah?" Ruth gasped, unable to believe what she was seeing. "What's going on?"

Hannah's eyes met Ruth's, filled with a mixture of shame and defiance. "I... I had to," she choked out. "You don't understand. My *familye*, we're going to lose everything!"

Daniel's grip on Hannah's arm loosened slightly, his expression a mixture of disappointment and concern. "Hannah, what are you talking about? Why would you do this?"

The young woman's composure crumbled, and she burst into tears. "My *mamm* is so sick," she sobbed. "The medical bills... we can't afford them. The bank is going to take our farm. I didn't know what else to do!"

Ruth's heart ached for Hannah, even as she struggled to reconcile this desperate act with the quiet, hardworking girl she'd known for years. She stepped forward, gently placing a hand on Hannah's shoulder.

"Oh, Hannah," she said softly. "Why didn't you *kumm* to us for help?"

Hannah shook her head, her voice barely above a whisper. "We couldn't... *Daed* is too proud. He said we had to handle it ourselves. But I couldn't just stand by and watch us lose everything."

By now, a crowd had gathered, their faces a mixture of shock, disappointment, and sympathy. Ruth could hear the whispers starting, could feel the judgment beginning to form. She knew they needed to act quickly to prevent this from spiraling out of control.

"Daniel," she said, her voice low but firm. "We need to take Hannah to the elders. This isn't something we can handle on our own."

Daniel nodded, his expression grave. "You're right. Eli, can you help me escort Hannah? Ruth, can you find Bishop Stoltzfus and ask him to convene the elders?"

Ruth nodded, her mind already racing. As she hurried off to find the bishop, she couldn't help but wonder how this would affect their community.

Would they show mercy to Hannah, understanding the desperation that drove her actions? Or would they judge her harshly, seeing her theft as a betrayal of their most fundamental values?

As she explained the situation to a stunned Bishop Stoltzfus, Ruth found herself praying fervently. *Gott, guide us,* she thought. *Help us find a way to justice that's tempered with mercy. Show us how to heal our community in the face of this betrayal.*

The bishop's face was grim as he nodded. "I'll gather the elders immediately," he said. "We'll meet in the community hall. Bring Hannah there. I'll send someone for her *familye*"

As Ruth made her way back through the market, she could feel the change in the atmosphere. The joy and festivity had been replaced by a tense, hushed anticipation. She spotted Daniel and Eli leading a subdued Hannah towards the community hall and hurried to join them.

"Ruth," Daniel said as she fell into step beside him. "How did it go with the bishop?"

"They're convening now," she replied, her voice low. "Daniel, what are we going to do? This is so much bigger than just catching a thief."

Daniel's eyes met hers, filled with a mixture of deter-mination and compassion. "We'll face it together," he said softly. "Whatever happens, we'll find a way through this. Our community is strong. We've weathered storms before. Whatever happens next, we're in this together. Okay?"

She nodded, clinging to his strength even as doubt and confusion swirled within her. As the bishop began to speak, addressing the stunned community, Ruth found herself at a crossroads once again.

Her candles had been a success, proof that innovation could work within their traditional framework.

But now, faced with this betrayal from within their own community, would the elders retreat further into the old ways? Would her newfound voice be silenced before it truly had a chance to be heard?

As the night closed in around them, the cheerful glow of the market lights now seeming somehow mocking, Ruth sent up a silent prayer.

Gott, guide us, she thought desperately. *Show us the path forward. Help us find a way to honor our traditions while embracing the future. And please, give me the strength to stand firm in my convictions, even in the face of doubt and disapproval.*

With Hannah's sobs echoing in her ears and Daniel be-side her, Ruth steeled herself for whatever was to come. The Christmas market, which had started with such promise, was a crucible.

And in its fires, Ruth knew the future of their commu-nity – and her own place within it – would be forged, for better or for worse, anew again.

Chapter 12

The bishop spoke first, explaining the situation, and then opened the floor for community members to discuss. Many, mostly those who were fellow vendors or relatives of vendors, wanted financial recompense for the stolen items.

Sarah Hersh's son, his daughter Esther by his side, was visiting but allowed to speak. He was clearly heated and suggested immediate shunning until a path forward was determined. No one else voiced support for such a strong step, though. Then, it was Daniel's turn.

Daniel's heart pounded as he stood before the gathered community, his voice steady despite the nerves roiling in his stomach.

"Friends, neighbors," he began, scanning the sea of familiar faces, "we've come together on this holy night not to condemn, but to understand. To seek a path forward that honors both our values and our compassion."

The community meeting hall, usually a place of joyous gatherings and peaceful worship, now thrummed with tension. The scent of pine boughs and spiced cider, remnants of the Christmas Eve festivities abruptly halted, hung heavy in the air.

Daniel's gaze fell on Hannah Zook, huddled between her parents, her face a mask of shame and fear. Her *mamm* was teary-eyed. Her *daed*, grim-faced and stoic.

"We all know why we're here," Daniel continued, his voice carrying clearly through the hushed room. "Hannah's actions have shaken us. But before we rush to judgment, we must ask ourselves: what would *Gott* have us do?"

A murmur rippled through the crowd. Daniel caught sight of Ruth, her warm brown eyes meeting his with a mixture of support and anxiety. She gave him a small nod, bolstering his resolve.

"Our way of life is built on forgiveness," Daniel pressed on. "On second chances. Hannah made a mistake, *jah*. Many mistakes, in fact. But haven't we all, at some point, strayed from the path?"

Bishop Stoltzfus leaned forward, his brow furrowed. "Daniel," he said, his deep voice cutting through the whispers, "we appreciate your desire for mercy. But repeated thefts like this are a serious matter. How can we trust Hannah after what she's done?"

Daniel took a deep breath, choosing his words carefully. "Trust must be rebuilt, that's true. But consider this: Hannah didn't steal out of greed or malice. She was desperate to save her *familye's* farm, to care for her ailing *mamm*."

He turned to Hannah, his voice softening. "Hannah, would you like to speak? To help us understand?"

Hannah rose shakily, her eyes red-rimmed from crying. "I... I know what I did was wrong," she began, her voice barely above a whisper. "I've betrayed your trust, and I'm so sorry. But I didn't know what else to do. *Mamm's* medical bills keep piling up, and with the mortgage, the bank..."

She choked back a sob. "A banker came by the other day. They're going to take our farm. Everything my *familye's* worked for, gone."

A hush fell over the room as Hannah's words sank in. Daniel saw looks of sympathy flash across many faces, though others remained stern and unyielding.

"This doesn't excuse your actions," Eli Yoder said firmly. "But it does shed light on the circumstances. Daniel, what do you propose we do?"

Daniel squared his shoulders, feeling the weight of the moment. "I believe Hannah should make amends through service to our community. Let her work to repay what she's taken, not just in money, but in trust. And in turn, let us come together to help the Zook *familye* in their time of need."

Ruth stood then, her quiet voice carrying a strength that made Daniel's heart swell with pride. "I support Daniel's proposal," she said. "I've known Hannah for years. She's always been kind and hardworking. This... this isn't who she truly is."

The room erupted in discussion, some voicing agreement while others argued for stricter punishment. Daniel watched as the elders huddled together, their expressions grave as they deliberated.

Finally, Bishop Stoltzfus raised his hand for silence. "We've heard the community's words. As well as from those most impacted, including the vendors. Your words, Daniel, and yours, Ruth, I find especially moving. After careful consideration, we agree to your proposal, with some additions."

He turned to Hannah. "You will work to repay what you've stolen, through service to those you've wronged and to the community at large. You'll also meet regularly with the elders for guidance and accountability."

Hannah nodded vigorously, tears of relief streaming down her face. "*Danki*," she whispered. "I'll do whatever it takes to make this right."

The bishop continued, addressing the community. "As for the Zook *familye's* struggles, we will *kumm* together to help them. It's clear we've failed in our duty to notice and aid a *familye* in need." He fixed Joseph Zook with a steady look. "Let this be a lesson to us all."

Daniel felt a wave of relief wash over him. It wasn't a perfect solution, but it was a start. As the meeting concluded with a communal prayer, he couldn't help but feel a sense of pride in his community. They had faced a difficult test and chosen the path of compassion.

As people began to file out of the hall, Daniel made his way to Hannah and her parents. "Are you all right?" he asked gently.

Hannah's *mamm*, nodded solemnly, gray faced. "We can't thank you enough, Daniel. For speaking up for our Hannah, for helping the community understand."

"It's what any of us would do," Daniel replied, though he knew that wasn't entirely true. Many would have chosen a harsher path.

Hannah looked up at him, her eyes shining with gratitude. "I won't let you down, Daniel. I promise."

Daniel smiled, squeezing her shoulder reassuringly. "I know you won't, Hannah. And remember, you're not alone in this. We're all here to support you."

As the Zook family moved away, Ruth appeared at Daniel's side. "You did *gut*," she said softly, her hand brushing his at their sides for the barest second.

Daniel felt a warmth spread through him at her touch. "We did *gut*," he corrected. "Your words made a difference, Ruth. You helped them see Hannah as a person, not just her mistakes."

Ruth's cheeks flushed at his praise. "I just spoke the truth. But, Daniel, what happens now? How do we move forward from this?"

Daniel sighed, running a hand across his chin. "One day at a time, I suppose. We'll need to work together to help the Zooks, to make sure Hannah has the support she needs to make things right."

As they walked out into the crisp December night, Daniel couldn't help but marvel at how differently this Christmas season turned out from what he'd expected. The stars twinkled overhead, reminding him of the first Christmas, of the hope and redemption it represented.

"You know," he said thoughtfully, "this is exactly what Christmas is about. New beginnings, coming together as a community."

Ruth nodded, her eyes reflecting the starlight. "*Jah*, I think you're right. It's not always easy, but it's what we're called to do."

They paused at the crossroads where they would part ways. Daniel turned to Ruth, suddenly feeling a bit shy. "Would you... would you like to *kumm* over tomorrow? For a Christmas Eve luncheon? My *familye* would love to have you."

Ruth's smile lit up her face. "I'd like that very much, Daniel."

As they said their goodnights, Daniel felt a sense of peace settle over him. The road ahead wouldn't be easy, but he was confident that their community would emerge stronger for having faced this challenge together.

He sent up a silent prayer of thanks as he walked home, his mind already whirling with ideas for how to help the Zooks and support Hannah in her journey of redemption. This Christmas had brought unexpected trials, but it had also reaffirmed his faith in his community and in the power of compassion.

The lights of his family's farmhouse came into view, warm and welcoming. Daniel quickened his pace, eager to share the events of the evening with his parents and siblings. As he stepped onto the porch, he paused for a moment, taking in the quiet beauty of the night.

"Merry Christmas," he whispered to the stars, bright purpose and hope for the future warming his chest. Whatever challenges lay ahead, he knew they would face them together, as a community united in faith and love.

The next morning dawned bright and clear, a blanket of fresh snow glistening in the early light. Daniel rose early, as was his habit, but today felt different. The events of the previous night had left him with a mixture of emotions - relief, hope, and a deep sense of responsibility.

As he made his way downstairs, the scent of his *mamm's* cinnamon rolls filled the air, a Christmas tradition that never failed to bring a smile to his face. His family was already gathered in the kitchen, their voices a comforting hum of conversation.

"*Gut* morning," he said, accepting a steaming mug of coffee from Sarah. "Merry almost Christmas."

His *daed* looked up from the newspaper, his eyes twinkling. "Merry almost Christmas, *Sohn*. How are you feeling after last night's meeting?"

Daniel sighed, sliding into his usual seat at the table. "It was... intense. But I think we made the right decision. Hannah deserves a chance to make things right."

His *mamm* nodded approvingly as she set a plate of cinnamon rolls on the table. "It's not always easy to choose mercy over judgment. You did *gut*, Daniel."

As they bowed their heads for the morning prayer, Daniel felt a surge of gratitude for his family's unwavering support. When he'd first started voicing his more progressive ideas, he'd worried they might not understand. But they had stood by him, even when it wasn't easy.

After breakfast, while they were cleaning up, his sister nudged him playfully. "So, I heard Ruth's coming over," she teased. "Anything you want to tell us, *Bruder*?"

Daniel felt his ears redden. "It's not like that," he protested weakly. "We're just friends."

His *mamm* and Sarah exchanged knowing looks, but mercifully dropped the subject. As much as Daniel treasured Ruth's friendship and support, he wasn't quite ready to examine the deeper feelings that had been growing between them.

The morning passed in a flurry of activity as they prepared for the day's festivities. Daniel found his thoughts drifting to Hannah and her family. He wondered how they were faring on this Christmas Eve morning, if the weight of recent events had cast a shadow over their holiday.

Just before noon, as his *mamm* was putting the finishing touches on their feast, Daniel made a decision. "I'm going to check on the Zooks," he announced, reaching for his coat. "I won't be long."

His *daed* nodded approvingly. "That's a *gut* idea, *Sohn*. Give them our best wishes."

The walk to the Zook farm was peaceful, the crunch of snow under his boots the only sound breaking the stillness. As he approached the farmhouse, Daniel noted with a pang how run-down it looked. The peeling paint and sagging roof were stark reminders of the family's struggles.

He knocked on the door, his breath forming small clouds in the frosty air. After a moment, Hannah's father, Joseph, answered. His eyes widened in surprise.

"Daniel? What brings you here on Christmas Eve?"

"I wanted to check on you all," Daniel said, suddenly feeling a bit awkward. "To see how you're doing after... everything."

Joseph's harsh expression softened. "That's... kind of you. Please, *kumm* in."

The interior of the house was warm, but Daniel couldn't help but notice the sparse furnishings and worn carpets. Hannah and her mother were seated by the fireplace, both looking up with startled expressions when he entered.

"Daniel," Hannah said, her voice barely above a whisper. "I... we weren't expecting anyone."

He smiled, trying to put them at ease. "I hope I'm not intruding. I just wanted to see how you were all doing, and to wish you a Merry Christmas."

Hannah's mother, Elizabeth, managed a weak smile. "That's very thoughtful of you, Daniel. We're... managing."

Daniel could see the strain on her face, and the toll her illness had taken. He set his shoulders back. He would help this family however he could.

"I know things are difficult right now," he said, addressing all of them. "But I want you to know that you're not alone. The community is here for you. We'll find a way through this together."

Hannah's eyes filled with tears. "After what I did... I don't deserve your kindness."

Daniel shook his head firmly. "That's not true, Hannah. We all make mistakes. What matters is how we learn from them and move forward."

He spent a few more minutes with the family, discussing ideas for how Hannah could begin her community service and ways they might be able to address their financial struggles. As he prepared to leave, he felt a glimmer of hope. It wouldn't be easy, but he believed they could find a path forward.

Back at home, Daniel found Ruth had already arrived. She was in the kitchen with his *mamm* and Sarah, her cheeks flushed from laughter as they prepared the final dishes for their feast.

"Daniel!" Ruth exclaimed, her eyes lighting up as she saw him. "Where have you been?"

He explained his visit to the Zooks, watching as understanding and admiration filled Ruth's expression. "That was very kind of you," she said softly.

As they all sat down to their meal, Daniel felt a deep sense of contentment. Yes, their community faced challenges. Yes, there were still hurdles to overcome.

But looking around the table at the faces of his loved ones, hearing the laughter and conversation, he knew that together, with *Gott's* grace and strength and wisdom, with the flame of faith alive in their hearts, they could weather any storm.

The meal was taken with stories and shared memories, the atmosphere warm and joyous. Daniel found his gaze continually drawn to Ruth, marveling at how naturally she fit in with his family. Her quiet strength and compassion had been a beacon throughout the recent troubles, and he realized with sudden clarity how much she had come to mean to him.

As the afternoon drew to a close, Daniel walked Ruth home. The day was clear and cold, the early sunset already giving way to twilight as the first stars twinkled overhead like diamonds scattered across the sky.

"Thank you for coming today," he said, his breath forming small clouds in the frosty air. "It meant a lot to have you there."

Ruth smiled up at him, her cheeks pink from the cold. "I'm glad I came. Your *familye* is wonderful, Daniel." They walked in comfortable silence for a few moments before Ruth spoke again. "What you did for the Zooks today... it was beautiful. You have such a kind heart."

Daniel felt a warmth spread through him that had nothing to do with the cold. "I just did what anyone would do," he said modestly.

Ruth shook her head. "Not anyone. You, Daniel. You see the best in people, even when they can't see it in themselves."

They had reached Ruth's house, but neither seemed eager to part. Daniel turned to face her, suddenly feeling nervous. "Ruth, I... I've been thinking. About us."

Her eyes widened slightly, but she remained silent, waiting for him to continue.

"You've become such an important part of my life," he said softly. "Your support, your wisdom... I don't know what I'd do without you. And I was wondering if... if you might consider allowing me to court you. I.. I know I'm not... I'm not doing it properly, a-and I *will* ask your parents, but do you... would you-"

Ruth's face broke into a radiant smile. "Oh, Daniel," she breathed. "I was hoping you'd ask. *Jah*, I'd like that very much."

For a moment, they just stood there, grinning at each other. Then, mindful of propriety, Daniel took Ruth's hand and gave it a gentle squeeze.

"*Gut* night, Ruth," he said softly. "And Merry Christmas."

"Merry Christmas, Daniel," she replied, her eyes shining.

While he walked home, Daniel's heart felt lighter than it had in weeks. The challenges they faced as a community were far from over, but he felt ready to face them head-on. With Ruth by his side and the support of their friends and neighbors, he believed they could build a brighter future for everyone in their little corner of Bird-in-Hand.

The stars twinkled overhead, reminding him of the hope and promise of that first Christmas so long ago. As Daniel whispered a prayer of thanks, a purposefulness washed over him. Whatever the new year might bring, he was ready to face it with faith, compassion, and love.

Chapter 13

Daniel's palms were sweating as he stood on the Brennemans' front porch, his heart pounding like that of a runaway buggy horse. He shifted the carefully wrapped package from one arm to the other, wiping his free hand on his trousers before reaching up to knock. The rich scent of roasted turkey and freshly baked pies wafted through the air, reminding him of the Christmas feast he'd left behind at his own home.

The door swung open, revealing Ruth's smiling face. "Daniel!" she exclaimed, her eyes lighting up. "I wasn't expecting you. Merry Christmas!"

"Merry Christmas, Ruth," Daniel replied, feeling a warmth spread through his chest at the sight of her. "I hope I'm not intruding on your *familye* celebration."

Ruth shook her head, ushering him inside. "*Nee*, not at all. We've just finished dinner. *Kumm* in, *kumm* in."

Daniel stepped into the cozy farmhouse and caught sight of Ruth's parents in the living room. Mr. Brenneman's brow furrowed slightly at his unexpected arrival, while Mrs. Brenneman offered a polite, if somewhat reserved, smile.

"*Gut* afternoon, Mr. and Mrs. Brenneman," Daniel said, his voice steadier than he felt. "I hope you're having a blessed Christmas."

"*Jah*, we are," Mr. Brenneman replied, setting aside the book he'd been reading. "What brings you here on Christmas Day, Daniel?"

Daniel took a deep breath, steeling his nerves. "Actually, sir, I was hoping I could speak with you and Mrs. Brenneman privately. If that's all right."

Ruth's parents exchanged a glance, a mixture of curiosity and concern passing between them. After a moment, Mrs. Brenneman nodded. "Of course, Daniel. Why don't we step into the kitchen?"

As they moved towards the kitchen, Daniel caught Ruth's eye. She gave him an encouraging smile, though he could see the question in her gaze. He wanted nothing more than to tell her everything, but he knew he had to do this right.

Once in the kitchen, Daniel set his package on the table and turned to face Ruth's parents. The tick of the old clock on the wall seemed impossibly loud in the sudden silence.

"Mr. and Mrs. Brenneman," he began, his voice low but clear, "I've *kumm* here today to ask for your blessing. I... I'd like to court your *dochder*, Ruth."

The words hung in the air for a moment. Mrs. Brenneman's eyes widened slightly, while Mr. Brenneman's expression remained unreadable.

"I see," Mr. Brenneman said slowly. "And what makes you think you're suitable for our Ruth?"

Daniel swallowed hard but pressed on. "Sir, I know I might not be the most traditional young *mann* in our community. But I care deeply for Ruth. We share the same faith, the same values. We work well together, and she... she brings out the best in me."

Mrs. Brenneman leaned forward, her brow creased with concern. "Daniel, we've heard about some of your... progressive ideas. The online store, wanting to use that to sell to the *Englisch*. How can we be sure you won't lead Ruth away from our ways?"

"I understand your concerns," Daniel said earnestly. "But my ideas aren't about abandoning our faith or our traditions. They're about finding ways to strengthen our community, to help us thrive in a changing world. Ruth helps me see how to balance progress with respect for our heritage."

Mr. Brenneman nodded slowly, considering Daniel's words. "And what about Ruth's shyness? Her struggles with confidence? How will you support her?"

Daniel felt a surge of protectiveness at the mention of Ruth's challenges. "I've seen Ruth grow so much in the short time we've been working together," he said softly. "She's stronger than she knows. I want to encourage her, to help her find her voice. But I also respect her gentle nature. It's one of the things I love most about her."

At the word "love," both of Ruth's parents straightened. Mrs. Brenneman's expression softened slightly, while Mr. Brenneman's eyes narrowed.

"Love is a serious word, Daniel," Mr. Brenneman said gravely. "Are you certain of your feelings?"

Daniel nodded, his heart pounding but his voice was steady. "*Jah*, I am. I love Ruth with all my heart. She balances me, challenges me to be better. I can't imagine my future without her by my side."

Just then, a soft gasp from the doorway caught their attention. They turned to see Ruth standing there, her eyes wide and shining with unshed tears.

"Ruth," Daniel breathed, feeling a mixture of joy and nervousness at her presence. "I... I wanted to surprise you."

Ruth stepped into the kitchen, her gaze never leaving Daniel's face. "Is it true?" she asked softly. "Everything you just said?"

Daniel nodded, reaching out but restraining himself from taking her hand. Her parents were right there, after all.

"Every word," he vowed. "Ruth, I love you. I want to court you properly, with your parents' blessing."

Ruth's face broke into a radiant smile. "Oh, Daniel," she whispered. "I love you, too."

They stood there for a moment, lost in each other's eyes until Mr. Brenneman cleared his throat.

"Well," he said, his voice gruff but not unkind, "I think your *mamm* and I need to discuss this privately."

Mrs. Brenneman nodded, gesturing for Ruth and Daniel to wait in the living room, out of hearing but still in sight. As the young couple left the kitchen, Daniel could hear the murmur of Ruth's parents' voices but couldn't make out their words.

In the living room, Ruth turned to Daniel, her eyes shining. "I can't believe you did this," she said softly. "Coming here on Christmas Day, talking to my parents..."

Daniel smiled. "I couldn't wait any longer," he admitted. "After everything we've been through with the market and Hannah... I realized life's too short to waste time. I want to build a future with you, Ruth."

Ruth's cheeks flushed pink, but her smile was radiant. "I want that too," she whispered. "But what if my parents say *nee*?"

Daniel smiled at her reassuringly. "Then we'll find a way to change their minds. Together."

The minutes ticked by slowly as they waited for Ruth's parents to emerge from the kitchen. Daniel found himself fidgeting with the buttons on his coat, while Ruth twisted her apron strings nervously.

Finally, the kitchen door opened. Mr. and Mrs. Brenneman stepped into the living room, their expressions unreadable. Daniel and Ruth stood, his hands clasped behind his back, hers tightly in front of her.

Mr. Brenneman cleared his throat. "Daniel, Ruth," he began, his voice solemn. "We've given this a lot of thought. And while we still have some concerns..."

Daniel held his breath, feeling Ruth tense beside him.

"...we can see how much you care for each other," Mrs. Brenneman finished, a small smile playing at the corners of her mouth. "We give you our blessing to court."

Ruth let out a joyful laugh, throwing her arms around her parents. "Oh, *Danki*!" she exclaimed. "*Danki* so much!"

Daniel felt a wave of relief and happiness wash over him. He shook Mr. Brenneman's hand firmly, then turned to Mrs. Brenneman, who surprised him with a warm hug.

"Take care of our girl," she whispered in his ear.

"I will," Daniel promised, his voice thick with emotion. "With everything I have."

As Ruth's parents stepped back, Daniel remembered the package he'd brought. "Oh! I almost forgot," he said, retrieving it from the kitchen.

He handed it to Ruth with a shy smile. "Merry Christmas, Ruth."

Ruth carefully unwrapped the gift, gasping softly as she revealed a beautifully carved wooden box. The lid was inlaid with a delicate pattern of flowers and vines, surrounding the words "Faith, Hope, Love" in an elegant script.

"Daniel," Ruth breathed, running her fingers over the smooth wood. "It's beautiful. Did you make this?"

He nodded, pleased by her reaction. "I did. Open it."

Inside, nestled on a bed of soft fabric, was a small, intricately carved wooden heart. Ruth lifted it out, her eyes widening as she saw the inscription on the back: "To Ruth, my heart's keeper. Love, Daniel."

Tears welled up in Ruth's eyes as she clutched the heart to her chest. "Oh, Daniel," she whispered. "I love it. I love you."

Mr. Brenneman cleared his throat, reminding them of his and Mrs. Brenneman's presence. "Why don't we all sit down?" he suggested. "We can have some pie and talk about your plans for courting."

As they settled in the living room with Mrs. Brenneman bringing out slices of her famous shoofly pie, Daniel felt a sense of peace settle over him. This was where he belonged, with Ruth and her family, blending their traditions with the promise of a bright future.

The conversation flowed easily as they discussed the parameters of the courtship. Daniel assured Ruth's parents that he would respect their rules and the community's expectations. They talked about their shared dreams for the future - a home filled with love and laughter, a thriving business that honored their Amish heritage while embracing thoughtful progress.

As the evening wore on, Daniel noticed Ruth stifling a yawn. Realizing how late it had grown, he reluctantly stood to leave. "I should be getting home," he said. "My *familye* will be wondering where I've disappeared to."

Ruth walked him to the door, her parents discreetly remaining in the living room to give them a moment of privacy. On the porch, illuminated by the soft glow of the lantern, Daniel boldly took both of Ruth's hands in his.

"I can hardly believe this is real," Ruth said softly, gazing up at him with shining eyes.

Daniel smiled, gently squeezing her hands. "It's real, Ruth. And it's just the beginning."

He leaned down, pressing a soft, chaste kiss to her forehead. As he pulled back, he saw Ruth's cheeks flush pink, a shy smile playing at her lips.

"*Gut* night, Daniel," she whispered. "And Merry Christmas."

"Merry Christmas, Ruth," he replied, his heart full to bursting. "I'll see you soon."

As Daniel made his way home through the crisp winter night, he couldn't stop smiling. The stars twinkled overhead, reminding him of the first Christmas and the hope it had brought to the world. Now, he felt that same hope blossoming in his own heart.

He sent up a silent prayer of thanks, grateful for the blessings of this day. Whatever challenges lay ahead, he knew he could face them with Ruth by his side. Together, they would build a life that honored their faith and traditions while embracing the future with open hearts and minds.

The lights within his family's farmhouse came into view, warm and welcoming. Daniel quickened his pace, eager to share the joyful news with his parents and siblings. As he stepped onto the porch, he paused for a moment, taking in the quiet beauty of the night.

"Merry Christmas," he whispered to the stars, feeling a renewed sense of purpose and hope for the future. This Christmas had brought an unexpected gift - the promise of a life shared with Ruth. And Daniel couldn't wait to see what the new year would bring.

Chapter 14

I n late January, Ruth's hands trembled slightly as she lifted the pot of molten wax from the stove. The familiar scent of beeswax and lavender filled her workshop, but not even the comforting aroma could quell the butterflies in her stomach. She took a deep breath, steadying herself before turning to face the small group gathered around her worktable.

"Now, we'll carefully pour the wax into the molds," she explained, her voice stronger than she'd expected. "Remember to leave a little space at the top for the wax to settle."

As she demonstrated the technique, Ruth couldn't help but marvel at how much had changed in just a few short weeks. Here she was, teaching her very first candle-making class, sharing her passion with others. The thought both thrilled and terrified her.

Hannah Zook caught her eye from across the table, offering an encouraging smile. Ruth felt a wave of warmth wash over her. Hannah had been one of the first to sign up for her class, eager to learn a new skill as part of her journey of redemption. Seeing her friend's progress filled Ruth with a sense of pride and hope.

As the students began pouring their own candles, Ruth moved around the table, offering guidance and encouragement. She paused beside an older woman who was frowning at her mold.

"Is everything all right, Mrs. Stoltzfus?" Ruth asked gently.

The woman sighed. "I'm not sure I'm cut out for this, Ruth. My hands aren't as steady as they used to be."

Ruth placed a comforting hand on Mrs. Stoltzfus's shoulder. "*Nee*, don't say that. Here, let me show you a trick."

She demonstrated how to brace the pouring pot against the edge of the mold, creating a steadier pour. Mrs. Stoltzfus's face lit up as she successfully filled her mold.

"Oh, Ruth!" she exclaimed. "That's much better. *Danki*."

As the class wound down, Ruth felt a surge of satisfaction. She'd done it. She'd actually taught others her craft, and they seemed to have enjoyed it. The students filed out, offering thanks and compliments, and leaving Ruth to tidy the workspace.

Hannah lingered behind, helping to clean up. "That was wonderful, Ruth," she said softly. "You're a natural teacher."

Ruth felt her cheeks warm at the praise. "*Danki*, Hannah. I'm just glad everyone seemed to enjoy it."

"They did," Hannah assured her. "And... well, I wanted to thank you. For including me in this. For giving me a chance."

Ruth's heart swelled with compassion. She reached out, squeezing Hannah's hand. "You're my friend, Hannah. We all make mistakes. What matters is how we learn and grow from them."

Hannah's eyes glistened with unshed tears. "I don't know what I'd do without friends like you and Daniel. You've both been so kind, so supportive."

As if summoned by the mention of his name, a knock sounded at the workshop door. Daniel poked his head in, his face breaking into a wide smile when he saw Ruth.

"There's my favorite candle maker," he said warmly. "How did the first class go?"

Ruth felt her heart skip a beat at the sight of him. Even after weeks of courtship, Daniel's presence still sent a thrill through her. "It went well, I think," she replied, unable to keep the pride from her voice. "Everyone seemed to enjoy it."

Daniel stepped into the workshop, nodding a greeting to Hannah. "I had no doubt you'd be amazing," he said, his eyes twinkling. "Are you ready for our meeting with Mr. Lapp?"

Ruth nodded, excitement bubbling up inside her. They were meeting with the shopkeeper to discuss selling their joint creations - her scented candles in Daniel's hand-carved holders. It was a perfect blend of their talents, and Ruth couldn't wait to see where this new venture might lead.

He didn't have an online store, but that didn't bother Ruth or Daniel. Just sharing their creations with more people was what they both wanted, and Mr. Lapp's storefront presented a perfect opportunity to do that.

And Mike and Linda wrote a letter, planning to visit Bird-in-Hand during springtime for a big buyer's trip. Linda described something called an "Etsy Shop" she was starting, so Daniel's dream of selling their work across the country and across the world might yet come true.

"I should go," Hannah said, sensing the couple's eagerness to be alone. "Ruth, thank you again for the class. I'll see you at the community gathering tonight?"

Ruth nodded, giving her friend a warm smile. "*Jah*, we'll be there. Take care, Hannah."

As Hannah left, Daniel wrapped his arms around Ruth, pulling her close. "I'm so proud of you," he murmured, pressing a soft kiss to her forehead. "You're really coming into your own, Ruth."

Ruth leaned into his embrace, savoring the moment. "I couldn't have done it without your encouragement," she said softly. "You make me believe in myself."

Daniel pulled back slightly, his blue eyes meeting hers. "You've always had this strength inside you, Ruth. I'm just glad you're finally letting it shine."

They stood there for a moment, lost in each other's gaze. Ruth marveled at how natural it felt to be in Daniel's arms, how right. But a glance at the clock on the wall brought her back to reality.

"We should go," she said reluctantly. "We don't want to be late for our meeting."

Daniel nodded, releasing her but keeping hold of her hand. As they walked out into the crisp January air, Ruth couldn't help but feel a sense of anticipation. This meeting could be the start of something wonderful for them both.

The bell above the door jingled merrily as they entered Lapp's General Store. Mr. Lapp, a jovial man with a salt-and-pepper beard, greeted them warmly.

"Ah, Ruth and Daniel!" he exclaimed. "I've been looking forward to this meeting. Come, let's see what you've brought."

Ruth carefully unwrapped the samples they'd prepared. Her hands shook slightly as she arranged the candles in their exquisite wooden holders on Mr. Lapp's desk.

"Oh my," Mr. Lapp breathed, leaning in for a closer look. "These are truly beautiful. The craftsmanship on both the candles and the holders is exceptional."

Ruth felt a surge of pride at his words. She glanced at Daniel, who was beaming with satisfaction.

"We were hoping you might be interested in selling them here in the store," Daniel explained. "We believe they'd appeal to both our community and the *Englisch* tourists."

Mr. Lapp nodded thoughtfully, picking up one of the candle holders to examine it more closely. "I agree. These would be perfect for our shop. The blend of traditional craftsmanship with a modern twist... it's exactly what our customers are looking for."

Ruth's heart soared. She'd been so nervous about this meeting, worried that their creations might be seen as too unconventional. But Mr. Lapp's enthusiasm was unmistakable.

"How many can you produce?" Mr. Lapp asked, his eyes twinkling with excitement.

Daniel and Ruth exchanged glances. "We can start with a small batch," Daniel suggested. "Say, twenty-five units? That would give us time to gauge interest and adjust production as needed."

Mr. Lapp nodded approvingly. "That sounds perfect. I'll take all twenty-five to start. If they sell as well as I think they will, we can discuss a larger order for the tourist season."

As they hammered out the details of their agreement, Ruth felt a sense of wonder wash over her. This was really happening. She and Daniel were starting a business together, combining their talents in a way that honored their ethos while embracing new possibilities.

When they left the store, contract in hand, Ruth could hardly contain her excitement. "I can't believe it," she said, her voice filled with awe. "He loved them, Daniel! And he wants to order more for the tourist season!"

Daniel grinned, pulling her close. "Of course he did. Your candles are amazing, Ruth. And together, we make quite a team."

Ruth's cheeks flushed at his praise. She still wasn't entirely used to this newfound confidence, but with Daniel by her side, she felt like anything was possible.

As they walked hand in hand towards the community hall for the evening gathering, Ruth's mind drifted to the future. Their spring wedding was only a few months away, and there was still so much to plan. But for now, she was content to live in this moment, savoring the joy of their shared success.

The community hall was already bustling when they arrived. Ruth felt a momentary flutter of nervousness as heads turned to watch them enter. It was still strange, being the center of attention as a courting couple. But the warm smiles and friendly greetings from their neighbors soon put her at ease.

They made their way through the crowd, stopping to chat with friends and family. Ruth's heart swelled to see Hannah sitting with a group of young women, laughing at something one of them had said. It was good to see her friend finding her place in the community once again.

"Ruth, Daniel!" a voice called out. They turned to see Sarah and Josiah Hersh waving them over. The quiltmaker was first in line to forgive Hannah, and even her son started coming around before he and his family went back home after New Year's Day.

"*Gut* evening," Ruth said as they approached. "How are you both?"

Sarah's eyes twinkled as she looked between Ruth and Daniel. "We're just fine, dear. But more importantly, how are you two? The whole community is buzzing about your courtship."

Ruth felt her cheeks warm, but Daniel squeezed her hand reassuringly. "We're doing well," he said, his voice filled with pride. "In fact, we just signed our first business contract today."

Josiah's eyebrows rose in interest. "Is that so? Tell us more."

As Daniel explained their new venture, Ruth found herself relaxing into the conversation. The Hershes listened attentively, asking thoughtful questions and offering words of encouragement.

"You know," Sarah said, her voice softening, "Josiah and I have been married for forty years now. And if there's one thing we've learned, it's that a strong partnership is the key to a happy marriage."

Josiah nodded in agreement. "*Jah*, and it looks like you two have already got that part figured out. Just remember to always communicate, even when it's difficult. And never go to bed angry."

Ruth felt a wave of gratitude wash over her. It meant so much to have the support and wisdom of their community behind them. "*Danki*," she said softly. "We'll remember that."

As the evening wore on, Ruth found herself reflecting on how much had changed in such a short time. Just a few months ago, she'd been too shy to even speak up at community gatherings. Now, here she was, confidently discussing her new business venture and her upcoming wedding.

Later, as she and Daniel took a quiet moment outside the hall, Ruth voiced her thoughts. "It's amazing, isn't it?"

she said, gazing up at the star-filled sky. "How much can change in such a short time?"

Daniel nodded, wrapping an arm around her shoulders. "*Jah*, it is. But you know what? I always knew you had this strength inside you, Ruth. I'm just glad everyone else gets to see it now too."

Ruth leaned into his embrace, feeling a sense of peace wash over her. "I couldn't have done it without you," she said softly. "You gave me the courage to believe in myself."

Daniel turned to face her, his eyes shining with love and pride. "You did that all on your own, Ruth. I just reminded you of what was already there."

Standing together under the stars, Ruth felt a surge of excitement for the future. In just a few short months, they would be husband and wife, starting their life together. There would be challenges, of course, but she knew that together, they could face anything.

"Daniel," she said, her voice barely above a whisper. "What do you think our life will be like? After we're married?"

He smiled, pulling her closer. "I think it will be wonderful," he said. "We'll have our home, our business. And someday, *Gott* willing, we'll have *kinner* running around. A whole houseful, underfoot and yelling and screaming. At least, if they take after me or Sarah," he said with a chuckle. "I wouldn't mind a few quiet *sohns* or *dochdern*, either."

Ruth's heart swelled at the thought. "I can't wait," she said softly.

"Neither can I," Daniel replied. He paused for a moment, then added, "You know, I've been thinking. Maybe we could expand the workshop, create a space where we can work on our projects together."

Ruth's eyes lit up at the idea. "Oh, Daniel, that would be perfect! We could have your woodworking tools on one side, my candle-making supplies on the other..."

As they continued to discuss their plans, Ruth felt a sense of excitement building within her. This was just the beginning of their journey together, and she couldn't wait to see where it would lead.

The sound of the gathering breaking up inside the hall brought them back to the present. "We should head back," Ruth said reluctantly. "It's getting late."

Daniel nodded, but before they went inside, he pulled her close for one more moment. "I love you, Ruth Brenneman," he said softly. "And I can't wait to spend the rest of my life with you."

Ruth's heart soared at his words. "I love you too, Daniel Fisher," she replied. "More than I ever thought possible."

They walked back into the hall, hand in hand, and Ruth felt a sense of completeness wash over her. She had found her voice, her passion, and the love of her life. Whatever the future held, she knew that with Daniel by her side and her faith to guide her, she could face anything.

The spring wedding might still be a few months away, but their life together had already begun. And Ruth could hardly wait to see what new wonders the days and years ahead would bring.

Chapter 15

Ruth exhaled slowly as she fastened the final pin in her prayer *kapp*, her reflection in the mirror showing a blend of nerves and excitement. The simple navy dress she wore, carefully sewn by her own hands, symbolized both her faith and the new chapter of life she was about to begin.

"You look beautiful, Ruth," Sarah said softly, adjusting the fall of Ruth's dress. "Daniel won't be able to take his eyes off you."

Ruth felt her cheeks warm at the compliment. She was glad Sarah could be with her, and more glad still her best friend pushed her to do the Christmas market in the first place.

And today, Sarah would become her sister, too. "*Danki*, Sarah. I can hardly believe this day is finally here."

The small room bustled with activity while Ruth's mother and other women helped make final preparations. The air was thick with excitement, a palpable energy that hummed through the very walls of the Brenneman home.

"Are you nervous?" Beth, Ruth's younger cousin, asked, her eyes wide with curiosity.

Ruth paused, considering the question. "A little," she admitted. "But mostly, I feel... ready. Like everything in my life has been leading to this moment. And I can't wait to see where we go together next."

Her mother stepped forward, tears glistening in her eyes. "Oh, my Ruth," she said, cupping her daughter's face in her hands. "You've grown into such a beautiful, strong young woman. Your *Daed* and I are so proud of you."

Ruth felt her own eyes well up, but she blinked back the tears, not wanting to ruin her appearance. "*Danki, Mamm*," she whispered, pulling her mother into a tight embrace.

As the women continued their preparations, Ruth's mind drifted to Daniel. Was he as nervous as she was? As excited?

She thought back to their courtship, to the challenges they'd faced and overcome together. From the market thefts to community skepticism about their ideas, they'd weathered every storm side by side.

A knock at the door interrupted her thoughts. "It's time," her father's voice called softly.

Ruth took a deep breath, smoothing her dress one last time. This was it. In just a few moments, she would walk outside, into the community hall, down the aisle, and begin her life as Ruth Fisher. Daniel's wife.

As she stepped out of the room, flanked by her mother and family and friends, a warm calm like a spring rain washed down over her. Whatever the future held, she was ready to face it.

With Daniel by her side, she could face anything.

The walk to the community hall was somehow endless, yet far too short. Ruth could hear the murmur of voices inside, the entire community gathered to witness their union. As they paused outside the doors, her father took her hand, giving it a gentle squeeze.

"Are you ready, mein *Liebling*?" he asked, his voice thick with emotion.

Ruth nodded, her heart swelling with love for her family and excitement for the future. "*Jah, Daed*. I'm ready."

The doors swung open, and Ruth stepped into her future, her eyes immediately finding Daniel's across the crowded room. His face lit up with a smile so bright it outshone the sun.

Without a doubt, this was exactly where she was meant to be. Ruth smiled back, brilliant and bright, taking the first step toward her love and their new life, their shining future.

Daniel's fingers fumbled with the buttons of his crisp, starched shirt, his nerves getting the better of him despite his best efforts to remain calm. He caught sight of his reflection in the small mirror hanging on the wall of the Fisher family's guest room, barely recognizing the man staring back at him.

"Need some help there, *Bruder*?" Eli, Daniel's younger brother asked with a grin. "Or are you trying to give yourself an excuse to be late to your own wedding?"

Daniel chuckled, shaking his head. "*Nee*, I think I can manage. Though I'm starting to wonder if these buttons have somehow gotten smaller since yesterday."

His father, John Fisher, stepped forward, his eyes twinkling with amusement and pride. "Here, let me," he said, gently brushing Daniel's hands aside to fasten the remaining buttons.

"I remember feeling just as nervous on my wedding day. Your *grossdaedi* had to practically push me out the door."

As his father worked, Daniel took a deep breath, trying to center himself. "I'm not nervous, exactly," he said, more to himself than to the others in the room. "Just... excited. And maybe a little overwhelmed."

Eli clapped him on the shoulder. "That's perfectly normal, Daniel. You're about to marry the love of your life. If you weren't feeling something, I'd be worried."

Daniel nodded, grateful for his family's support. As he shrugged on his black vest and jacket, his mind wandered to Ruth. Was she as anxious as he was? As eager to begin their life together?

"There," John said, stepping back to admire his handiwork. "You look every inch the groom, *mein Sohn*."

Daniel turned to face the mirror once more, hardly believing the transformation. The man looking back at him was no longer just Daniel Fisher, woodworker and dreamer. He was a husband-to-be, ready to take on the responsibilities and joys of marriage.

"Daniel," his father said softly, drawing his attention. "Before we go, I wanted to tell you how proud your *Mamm* and I are of you. You've grown into a fine *mann*, one who's not afraid to stand up for what he believes in. Ruth is lucky to have you."

Daniel felt a lump form in his throat. "I couldn't have done any of this without you and *Mamm*, especially. Sarah, too," he added with a laugh. "She's the one who brought us together at the market in the first place."

He glanced at Eli and said, "No thanks to you, though, *Bruder*."

Eli only laughed.

"So, *danki, Daed*," Daniel managed, pulling his father into a tight embrace.

As they broke apart, Eli cleared his throat. "Not to interrupt this touching moment, but we should probably get going. Unless you want Ruth to think you've changed your mind."

Daniel laughed, the tension in his shoulders easing slightly. "Not a chance," he said firmly. "Let's go."

The short buggy ride, then the walk to the community hall was a blur of well-wishes and excited greetings from neighbors and friends. Daniel's heart raced with each step, knowing that soon, he would see Ruth walking down the aisle towards him.

As they approached the hall, Daniel paused, taking in the scene before him. The entire community had come together to celebrate their union, the strength of their bonds evident in every aspect of the event.

He spotted Hannah Zook helping to arrange flowers near the entrance, her face alight with joy. Eli Yoder, once skeptical of Daniel's progressive ideas, offered a warm smile and a pat on the back as he passed.

"This is it," John said, giving Daniel's shoulder a squeeze. "Are you ready, *Sohn*?"

Daniel took a deep breath, squaring his shoulders. "*Jah*," he said, his voice steady and sure. "I've never been more ready for anything in my life."

As he stepped into the hall, the buzz of conversation quieted. Daniel made his way to the front, his eyes scanning the crowd for familiar faces. He saw friends and family, eyes shining with unshed tears. His own mother and sister sat in the front row, beaming with pride.

And then, suddenly, the doors at the back of the hall swung open. Daniel's breath caught in his throat as Ruth appeared, radiant in her simple, dark blue dress. Their eyes met across the crowded room, and in that moment, everything else faded away. It was just the two of them, ready to embark on the greatest adventure of their lives.

As Ruth made her way down the aisle, Daniel felt a sense of peace wash over him. This was right. This was where he was meant to be. And with Ruth by his side, he knew they could face anything life might throw their way.

Ruth's heart pounded as she took her first steps down the aisle, her eyes locked on Daniel's. The community hall, usually so familiar, seemed transformed into something magical. Sunlight streamed through the windows, casting a warm glow over the gathered friends and family.

As she walked, Ruth felt the weight of tradition in every step. Her simple dress, the prayer *kapp* carefully pinned to her hair, the expectant faces of the community – all of it spoke to the traditions of their faith, traditions she and Daniel would gladly continue.

But there was something else, too. A spark of new beginnings, of a future filled with possibilities. She saw it reflected in Daniel's eyes, in the way he stood tall and proud at the front of the hall, waiting for her.

When she finally reached him, Ruth felt like she'd come home. Daniel swayed toward her, his gaze warm and reassuring.

"You look beautiful," he whispered, his voice filled with awe.

The bishop began the ceremony, his words washing over Ruth in a comforting wave. She and Daniel's traditional wedding emphasized commitment, community, and faith.

While they exchanged their vows, Ruth's voice grew stronger with each word. This wasn't just a promise to Daniel, but to their entire community. To honor their heritage while embracing the future. To build a life together rooted in faith and love.

When the bishop finally pronounced them husband and wife, the hall erupted in joyous song. Ruth felt tears of happiness spring to her eyes as Daniel smiled at her, his own eyes shining with unshed tears of joy as well.

The reception that followed was a whirlwind of congratulations, shared meals, and laughter. Ruth was constantly amazed by the outpouring of love and support from their community. Even those who were once skeptical of their relationship now offered heartfelt blessings.

Hannah approached them during a lull in the festivities, her eyes shining. "I'm so happy for you both," she said, pulling Ruth into a tight hug. "You deserve all the joy in the world."

Ruth squeezed her friend's hand, remembering how far they'd all come. Months after the shocking Christmas revelations, Hannah and her family were fully forgiven, and the Zooks were welcomed into the embrace of the community. Her *daed* still struggled to accept help, but after the family attended multiple gatherings, hearing "Danki, Hannah. We couldn't have done this without you and the rest of the community," he quickly adapted to be accepting.

As the day wore on, Ruth found herself stealing quiet moments with Daniel whenever they could. During one such moment, as they stood near the edge of the gathering, Daniel stepped close to her.

"Can you believe it?" he murmured, his breath warm against her ear. "We did it. We're married."

Ruth laughed softly, her heart overflowing with happiness. "It still feels like a dream," she admitted. "But the best kind of dream – one I never want to wake up from."

Daniel's eyes sparkled as he gazed at her. "Well, Mrs. Fisher, I promise to do everything in my power to make sure this dream lasts a lifetime."

As the sun began to set, casting a golden glow over the festivities, Ruth and Daniel prepared to depart for their new home, built in the last month in between their parents' homes. The community gathered to see them off, showering them with well-wishes and cheers.

Ruth hugged her parents tightly, feeling a bittersweet pang at the thought of leaving her childhood home. "I love you both so much," she whispered, her voice thick with emotion.

Her mother cupped her face gently. "Go and build your new life, *mein Liebling*," she said softly. "But remember, you'll always have a home here."

As they climbed into the buggy, waving goodbye to their friends and family, Ruth felt a sense of excitement and anticipation wash over her. This was the beginning of their new life together – a life full of possibilities, challenges, and love.

Epilogue

The December wind nipped at Daniel's cheeks as he carefully arranged the last of their handcrafted items on the rustic shelves he'd built for their market stall. The scent of pine and snow hung in the air, mingling with the aroma of fresh-baked goods from nearby booths. He stepped back, admiring the display of wooden candle holders and intricately scented candles – a perfect blend of his and Ruth's talents.

"What do you think?" he asked, turning to Ruth with a grin. "Not bad for our first Christmas market as a married couple, eh?"

Ruth's eyes sparkled as she took in their handiwork. "It's perfect, Daniel. I can hardly believe how far we've *kumm* in just a year."

Daniel pulled her close, planting a kiss on her forehead. "And it's only the beginning, *Liebling*. Just wait and see what we can accomplish in the years to come."

As the market bustled to life around them, Daniel hardly believed all the changes the past year had wrought. Their wedding day felt both like yesterday and a lifetime ago. In the months since, they'd settled into their new home and expanded their business.

Hannah approached their booth, her arms laden with quilts. "*Gut* morning!" she called cheerfully. "Your display looks wonderful!"

Daniel beamed, taking in Hannah's bright smile and easy manner. It was hard to believe this was the same young woman who, less than a year ago, was caught stealing from the market. Her journey of redemption had been inspiring to watch, and he was proud to call her a friend.

"*Danki*, Hannah," Ruth replied warmly. "How are you feeling? Not too tired, I hope?"

Hannah laughed, patting her slightly rounded belly. "Oh, this little one keeps me up some nights, but I'm not complaining. Eli's been wonderful, taking on extra chores so I can rest."

Daniel shook his head in amazement. If someone had told him a year ago that Hannah and Eli would be married and expecting their first child, he would never have believed it. But life had a way of surprising you – usually for the better.

As the day progressed, Daniel found himself reflecting on all the changes in their community. The market, once plagued by thefts and suspicion, now thrived, more bustling than ever. His and Ruth's business had grown beyond their wildest dreams, with several monthly orders from Mr. Lapp's store, not to mention Mike and Linda in Philadelphia.

But more than the material successes, Daniel was grateful for the deeper bonds that had formed. The way the community had rallied around the Zooks family, especially Hannah, during that difficult time. The growing acceptance of some of his more progressive ideas was balanced with a deep respect for their traditions.

As the sun began to set, casting a dying glow over the market, Daniel and Ruth began packing up their unsold items. They worked in comfortable silence, moving in perfect sync – a dance they'd perfected over months of shared labor and love.

"What do you say we host a small gathering at our place on Christmas Eve?" Daniel suggested as they loaded the last box into their buggy. "Nothing fancy. To celebrate how far we've all *kumm* this year."

Ruth's face lit up at the idea. "Oh, Daniel, that would be wonderful! We could invite Hannah and Eli, and your *familye*, and mine..."

Daniel chuckled, pulling her close. "I love how your mind works, Mrs. Fisher. Always thinking of ways to bring people together."

As they made their way home through the crisp winter evening, Daniel sent up a silent prayer of thanks. For Ruth, for their community, and for the life they were building together. He knew there would be challenges ahead – there always were. But with Ruth by his side and their faith to guide them, he felt ready to face whatever the future might bring.

Ruth hummed softly as she placed the last of the Christmas cookies on a platter, the warm scent of cinnamon and nutmeg filling their cozy kitchen. Outside, the first flakes of snow were beginning to fall, blanketing their little corner of Bird-in-Hand in a soft white glow.

"Daniel?" she called, wiping her hands on her apron. "Can you help me move the table? I think we'll need the extra space for tonight."

Her husband appeared in the doorway, his face flushed from stoking the fire in the living room. "Of course, *Liebling*," he said with a smile. "Though I still think you might be overestimating how many people are coming to this 'small gathering' of ours."

Ruth laughed, shaking her head. "Better to have too much than not enough, right? Besides, you know how Hannah's eating for two lately."

As they worked together to rearrange the furniture, Ruth sighed happily. It was all so natural. This home they'd built together, the easy rhythm they'd fallen into as a married couple – this life was everything she'd ever dreamed of and more.

The sound of buggy wheels on gravel announced the arrival of their first guests. Ruth smoothed her dress, suddenly feeling a flutter of nerves. This was their first time hosting a gathering as a married couple, and she wanted everything to be perfect.

"Relax," Daniel said softly, sensing her tension. He placed a gentle kiss on her cheek. "Everyone's going to love it because they love us. And even if the cookies burn or the punch spills, it'll still be a wonderful evening."

Ruth took a deep breath, letting his words wash over her. "You're right," she said, squeezing his hand. "Let's go greet our guests."

The evening passed in a blur of laughter, good food, and heartfelt conversations. Ruth watched with joy as their small home filled with friends and family, all coming together to celebrate the season and the bonds that tied them.

Hannah and Eli arrived, their faces glowing with the excitement of expectant parents. Ruth's heart swelled as she remembered their journey – from the darkest days of Hannah's mistake to this moment of pure happiness.

"Ruth," Hannah said, pulling her aside at one point in the evening. "I just wanted to thank you again. For everything. I don't know where I'd be if you and Daniel hadn't stood by me last year."

Ruth felt tears prick at her eyes. "Oh, Hannah," she said softly. "You did all the hard work yourself. We just reminded you of the strength you already had inside."

As the night wore on, Ruth found herself taking mental snapshots of the scene around her. Daniel, deep in conversation with her father about some new woodworking technique. Her mother and Daniel's, swapping recipes and grandmotherly advice for Hannah. Eli, sitting next to his *fraa*, laughed at something Daniel's brother said.

This, she realized, was what it was all about. Not just the big moments like their wedding day, but these quiet, ordinary evenings filled with love and community.

When the last guest had departed and the house was quiet once more, Ruth and Daniel stood in the doorway, watching the snow continue to fall.

"Merry Christmas, Mrs. Fisher," Daniel murmured, pulling her close.

"Merry Christmas, Mr. Fisher," Ruth replied, her heart full to bursting. "Thank you for making all my dreams come true."

She tilted her head up as Daniel leaned down, their lips meeting in a perfect, familiar kiss.

Thank you so much for reading, I hope you
enjoyed the story!

**<u>Sign up for my newsletter for a free sto-
ry.</u>**

About Miriam Beiler

Want to connect?
Please feel free to visit my Facebook page:
https://www.facebook.com/miriambeilerauthor

Or email me: **miriam@miriambeiler.com**

Made in the USA
Middletown, DE
28 December 2024

68381027R00081